Til Death Do Us Part

Til Death Do Us Part

NICOLE MILNER

CONTENTS

Prologue

TIL DEATH DO US PART

I'm sitting here in this car, but my legs won't move. It's been five years. You can do it Caryn, you can do it. Man, you know going to a cemetery is never easy, no matter how many years have gone by. To some it's peaceful and calming, but to me it's just plain depressing. You stand there, you say a few words, you pray, you remember, you cry. A part of you hope that your loved one somehow someway can hear you, can feel you. Eerie, right?

It's hard to believe that I lost you five years ago today. As I celebrate my 40th birthday this year, it still haunts me that you never made it to see 40.

As I stand over this grave today, so many memories come flooding back like a raging river that had been held back by a dam; some good, some bad, some just downright painful. Lord knows if I could do things over differently, I would. If I could just turn back the clock, it would have changed the course of my life.

Ok girl, get it together! Leave these flowers on this grave, and get the hell out of here. What has happened has happened, and ain't nothing you can do about it. "Trust in the Lord with all your heart and do not lean on your own understanding."

1

SLOW JAM

Labor Day Weekend

I was excited to start my junior year at Pirate University. I had just broken up with my high school sweetheart for I know the 20th time, so I was looking forward to leaving home and his ass and going back to school. Of course Richmond would always be my home, but it was always a good feeling to be in Hampton. I was going to be staying with my Aunt Max again this school year, so I didn't have to worry about housing, trifling roommates and their boyfriends, and eating unknown substances with double portions of carbs at the caf.

Aunt Max was an excellent cook and was as cool as they come. We could talk about anything. She was divorced and had one child. She'd been through a lot during her life and was a wealth of knowledge. Aunt Max was my confidant, my friend.

I was feeling a bit down thinking about my high school sweetheart, so my girlfriend Monica and I decided to go to Virginia Beach to a concert in the park.

Monica and I met sophomore year in Business 101 class. She asked me if she could see my notes one day, and we've been friends every since. Monica was from Chicago, Chi-town. Our joke is that we bonded because she was from the southside of Chicago and I was from southside Richmond.

Monica and I were like night and day. I was organized and always on time, and let's just say she was not. She was spur of the moment, and I was the cautious one. She watched *All My Children*, and I watched *The Young and the Restless*. Somehow even with our differences, we clicked back then and became the best of friends.

It was Labor Day weekend, so we expected that guys from all over the east coast would be at the park. I put on a cute black and white bikini top and white shorts. "Be careful Caryn", my Aunt Max said as I rushed out the house. "I will Auntie Max," I yelled back. I met Monica at her apartment, and she drove us down to the beach. It was hot at Hades that day, but that didn't stop us from going. I don't think anything could have stopped us at that point. I just wanted to get away and have some fun; Monica wanted to hook up with some "fine guy." The thought of meeting some fine guy was the farthest thing from my mind, but I damn sure was open if the opportunity presented itself.

We had to leave our car at a lot and catch a shuttle over to the park. There were people everywhere. Guys were definitely trying to hit on us, but none of them made me look twice. Short, stocky, skinny, missing teeth, gold teeth, no teeth, bald, going bald, you name it and that's who tried to hit on us. It was rather funny then and it's still pretty funny now.

"Ok, Monica I am going to get something to eat. I want a hotdog. You want me to get you something?" I asked. Funny how when you are 20 years old you can eat and eat whatever the hell you want. You could eat two hotdogs and loose five pounds. In your 40's you ration your portions and stress over what you should and should not eat. You eat two hot dogs, gain ten pounds, and feel so bad you end up praying for forgiveness, going to confessional, or whatever it takes so you won't feel so guilty.

I went over to the hotdog stand and placed our order. The music was pumping in the background, and I was grooving to the beat. All of a sudden I heard this voice say, "Excuse me, are you with someone?"

I turned and looked up, and all I can say is my, my, my. Bingo! I think the fine guy finally found me. Tall (6'3 to be exact), handsome, confident, definitely smooth. After I got myself together, because I think I was in a bit of a shock, I responded, "Yes, with a girlfriend." He told me his name was Bernard and that he was at the park with his roommate Jay. Bernard politely asked my name and if he could walk me over to where we were sitting. "Hell yeah!" I wanted to say. But of course, I remained composed and said "Sure."

As I was introducing Bernard to Monica, his friend Jay had come over to where we were. Bernard told Jay that we were from Pirate U. Jay seemed to be interested in Monica, which worked for me because I wanted to hear more about this Bernard.

We talked what seemed like hours. They stayed with us until the concert was over. Bernard told me that he was 24 years old, was a contractor, never been married, and no kids. Sounded good so far.

We found out that we had a few things in common like we both were only children, had divorced parents, and we both had family in the Washington, DC area. He actually was born and raised in D.C., and had only been in Virginia a couple of years. It was easy talking to him. He seemed so mature. I guess to a 20 year old, talking to a guy four years older than you were did make him seem more mature. He had intrigued me and I wanted to know more.

At some point Jay said, "Come on ya'll we did pay for a show, let's dance." Even though we knew we could hear the music in the background, it almost seemed muted if that makes sense. We were so busy learning about each other, that we kind of forgot that there actually was a band playing.

Bernard grabbed my hand and pulled me up close to him. As he slowly and meticulously gyrated, my body followed his rhythm. Now the feeling that I got when my body was up against his was something that I had never quite felt before. You know that tingling feeling. The magnetism was a bit scary or maybe unfamiliar is a better word. Whatever it was, it felt good and intrigued me enough that I wanted to "feel" more. Slow jamming ain't never felt this good. Go head Mr. DJ, play another slow jam!

After the concert, Bernard and Jay walked us over to the shuttles. Bernard promised to call me sometime over the holiday weekend. Jay and Monica exchanged numbers too. Bernard kissed my hand and said, "It was my pleasure meeting you Caryn, and we will meet again. I promise you that." Ok, I liked to have fallen out right then but, not trying to loose cool points, I responded, "Me too. Enjoy the rest of your weekend Bernard."

2

ALL I DO IS THINK OF YOU

The next couple of weeks went by pretty fast. Classes started, football season was in, guys and girls were hooking up, and everything else that happens on campus in the fall of the year. Monica and Jay talked maybe a couple of times on the phone, but she said he was too arrogant for her. Bernard and I talked almost every night since we met at the park. He worked evenings so he would call me when he got off work around 12:30 in the morning. He would be at the pay phone near his job (Yes, a pay phone. That's what we used back then) and we would talk until sometimes 2:00 in the morning.

All I did was think of this man; how he looked, how he felt, how he made me feel. I couldn't wait until our first date. He told me to meet him at the beach one night after he got off work. I told my Aunt Max his name, gave her his phone number, and told her to call 911 if I wasn't back by 3:00 am. Let's be real, 12:30 in the morning was pretty late to be meeting some guy that you just met. I wasn't really scared, more like cautious. Probably the southside Richmond in me.

As soon as I parked, I saw him. Even with his work clothes on, he was still fine. He had that blue collar thang going on, and it took all I had not to jump his bones right then. "Hey Caryn, follow me," he said. We walked along the ocean holding hands and just enjoying the ocean breeze. Finally we sat on a bench and just talked and learned more about each other. We talked about our families. He talked a lot about his dad and his mom. I talked about Pirate University and how I wanted to pledge a sorority this year. He told me that he had gone to college on a basketball scholarship for about three years, but never finished. So, we also talked about college life.

We stayed a couple of hours, and then decided that we'd better get going since it was late. He gently kissed me good night, walked me to my car, and we parted. Bernard had a way of making you feel comfortable and at ease with him. He was a charmer and knew, even as a young man, how to get a woman into him. We had a really nice time together this first night, and it was a night that I never forgot.

The next day, I called Bernard and his roommate Jay told me that he wasn't there and that he would give him a message that I called. I realized that every time I would call Bernard, I either didn't get an answer or Jay would say he wasn't home. Bernard finally called me from the pay phone about three days later after he got off work. I asked him what was up with him not calling me back, and he told me that he needed to tell me something. He told me that he didn't live with Jay. He lived with his ex-girlfriend. He said that they were having problems and that he was planning on moving out. He was there for the most part to help her with her three year old and until he could get his own place.

So I said, "So you have been lying to me? You live with your girlfriend, and not Jay? "Oh no, Caryn. It's not like that at all sweetheart. I am looking for my own place, and she and I are not together," he assured me. "Why did you tell me that you were living with Jay and not your girlfriend, Bernard?" "Listen to me Caryn. I only told you that because I thought I would have my own place by that Tuesday after Labor Day weekend. Things fell through, so I have to wait a little longer. I never meant to lie to you. You mean a lot to me and so does our relationship."

I laid there that night thinking about what Bernard had said. It all started to make sense now. He had always called me from a pay phone late at night after work or from a friend's house. He had never called me from home. He had never invited me to his place either.

As a young twenty year old beginning to fall in love truly for the first time, I had no reason not to believe Bernard. The next day in class, I told Monica about Bernard's living arrangements. "What the fuck?" she said. "Well don't worry about it now girl, we gotta get ready for homecoming and all of those parties!"

3

THE CLOSER I GET TO YOU

Ahh, homecoming. Homecoming at Pirate U is usually mid fall so most of the time the weather is warm and just right. This time of year you could just sit by the glistening lake on campus among the falling autumn leaves. There's nothing like a HBCU homecoming. Just think of a fashion, hair, comedy, step, and cooking show all rolled up into one. One big party with mini little parties pretty much kind of sums it up.

Monica and I were both on the homecoming committee, and we were going to represent the committee on the float this year at the homecoming parade. I had planned to spend the weekend at her place, so I packed my overnight bag and was all set to go. My Aunt Max was a Hampton alumna, so she was getting ready for the homecoming weekend events too.

"Aunt Max, what are you doing after the game?" I asked. I think I already knew the answer to the question, but I was curious to see what she was going to say. "Well, since I have a babysitter for tonight and you will be gone for the weekend, let's just say I am going to enjoy some adult entertainment," was her response. "Well, make sure you have protection, like you always tell me," I said.

On that note, I left for Monica's place. Of course, she was not ready when I got there. We arrived on campus just in enough time to hop, and I mean hop, on the float right before the parade started. It was fun actually to see all the creativity and energy that everybody had put into building all of the floats. The fraternities and sororities, Mr. and Miss Pirate U, and all of the other organizations competed to have the best looking float.

It was a beautiful fall day. The fall foliage was a mixture of red, orange, and yellow. The campus was filled with laughter and excitement. Homecoming was like a family reunion. Greeks stepping on the yard, the aroma of grilled and fried food permeating throughout, alumni joking and reminiscing about old times, and college paraphernalia everywhere. And let's not forget guys, guys, and more guys.

After the parade, we grabbed something to eat and hung around on the yard until it was time for the game. As we were walking, I heard someone say, "Hey Caryn." I looked behind me, and it was Bernard. "Where did you come from? You stalking me?" I jokingly asked. "Remember I played basketball and football in high school and college too. I still like to see the young guys play." "So, you like to tackle, huh? Just how good are you at tack-ling?" I asked seductively. "Touchdowns baby all the way," he said with that sexy voice of his.

At this point, I had forgotten all about Monica. Looked like she had forgotten about me too because she was all up in some guy's face exchanging numbers. Bernard and I agreed to hook up sometime over the weekend. All this talk about tackling and touchdowns was making me a bit excited. I watched him walk on over to the football field. You would think he'd walk goofy because of his 6'3 frame, but that was not the case. Bernard had a smooth, confident walk; more like a gentle swagger.

The game was close, but we won. It's nothing more depressing than losing a homecoming game! The rest of the weekend went by pretty fast. Monica and I party hopped and finally got to bed around 3:00 Sunday morning.

Bernard met me at Monica's apartment Sunday evening around 4:00. He said he knew of a really good Chinese take-out place, so we decided to go there and grab dinner. While we were waiting for our order, I reminded him about how he talked about his "skills" in tackling and touchdowns. He rubbed my inner thigh and reminded me how ready he was to show me just how "good" he really was. It's a blur right now, but at some point we decided to take the food and check in to the nearest hotel room.

I had thought about this moment for weeks. My body had been craving Bernard since that very first time we danced. As soon as we got to the room, he kissed and caressed me all over with an intensity I have never experienced before. His touch made me explode and all I wanted at that moment was to feel him. He must have read my mind because he seemed to just glide inside me gently, confidently. I found his rhythm and our bodies joined for the very first time.

As we lay in each other's arms, we laughed and talked about a little bit of everything. Bernard told me that his mom had passed away a couple of years ago suddenly from a heart attack and how the news of her passing had affected him. Her passing was the reason why he moved to Virginia. The more we talked, the closer I felt to him. Being with Bernard that evening had changed me and how I felt about making love and being in love.

We left the hotel early the next morning. I had a morning class, and Bernard kept his ex-girlfriend's daughter during the day. When I got back to my Aunt Max's house, she was getting ready to go to work. We promised to catch up about our weekend at dinner, so she headed out the door while I got ready for class.

My psychology course was my favorite, and I was usually excited about going. With all of the events of homecoming weekend though, I could barely keep my eyes open in class. The morning seemed to last forever. I was done by 12:00, so I went straight home, ate lunch, and watched "The Young and the Restless." After my soaps went off, I took a nice long nap. Before I knew it, Aunt Max was home and my little ten year old cousin Michael came running into my room. "Caryn, what are you doing? Guess what? Mommy is making lasagna for dinner. I can't wait!" he said. "Ok, Michael I'll be down in a little bit, please shut my door." I slept for a little while longer, then I went downstairs to the kitchen.

"Ummm, something smells good! Aunt Max you have got to show me how to make lasagna." I sat in the kitchen with her while she prepared dinner. We talked about how we both spent homecoming weekend. I told her about seeing Bernard at the game, and how we hooked up on Sunday. "So, how do you feel?" Aunt Max asked. "Can you make lasagna for the wedding rehearsal dinner?" I said. "Now slow down a minute young lady. Don't go ringing the wedding bells just yet. Isn't Bernard still living with his so-called ex-girlfriend?" "Just until he finds his own place which will be in a few weeks. The point is I that had a wonderful time with him and I feel closer to him than I've ever felt to anyone. Be happy for me!" "You are still very young and vulnerable Caryn. Take your time and don't rush things. Bernard still has some things he needs to take care of at home," she said.

On that note, we all sat down for dinner. After I helped with the dishes, I went up to my room to study. It was hard to concentrate because I kept thinking about last night with Bernard. My mind would drift off to what it would be like on our wedding day. Ahh, remember young love? You have sex one time with a guy, and you automatically start planning the wedding in your head. What you realize though as you get older is that what you really had was not love, but just real good sex, period.

That spring, I competed to get on line for the sorority, well let's just call it "Beta Beta". I was really excited when I went to the rush. There were so many girls trying out for a spot of 50. I believe 300 actually showed up to the rush. I had been to the rush my sophomore year just to see what it was like. I knew then that I would be signing the book my junior year. I tried to get Monica to try with me, but she was like "Hell no! Ain't no sisterhood in degrading and being nasty to your so-called sisters. Thanks, but I'll pass."

Every since freshman year, I had been impressed with "Beta Beta". They had a seminar for us about freshman life on campus. They started off by doing their chant, "All I want to be is a Beta, Beta...." Although I think they would have killed you if they ever heard a non "Beta Beta" sing it, that tune had always stuck in my brain. My Aunt Max pleaded with me to join her sorority, but I told her my heart was in "Beta Beta". I think she was a bit disappointed, but she understood that it was my choice.

I was selected to go through the whole process of trying to make the line. I never forgot the talent show that we had to do for the sorority sisters. We only had an hour or so to come up with a group and individual show. Crazy me decided to rap! I was never one to be shy, and I figured that would be a way that I would stand out. I got a standing ovation believe it or not, and I went away that night feeling pretty confident that I was in.

Another big thing was going to or calling "the house." Some of the senior "Beta Beta's" lived in this particular house and whenever you called, you had to ask for all of them. So, I called this one time. I said, "Hello, this is Caryn and I'd like to speak to Tonya, Lisa, Michelle, and DD." The person on the phone yelled back, "How the hell you gonna speak to all of us? Call back later damnit." Needless to say, I never called back. I did however go with another girl, Carmen to the house about a week later. She was trying to make the line too. Carmen had to do some project for one of the "Beta Beta's" and was instructed to drop it off at the house at 11:00 that night. We were always told to never go anywhere alone, so I went with her to take this freaking project of hers.

Even though the "Beta Beta's" were expecting her, they were no lights on in the house nor were there any on the outside. It was dark, and my red flags went up. We rang the doorbell and knocked a couple of times, but nobody came. All I kept thinking was what if they let us in there and beat the crap out of us? All of a sudden we heard a scratching sound on the inside of the door and then a loud scream. We hauled ass and said the hell with that project! I must say they got us that night, because we were scared as hell.

I made it all the way to the final interview process. I was so excited, and couldn't wait to be snatched. About a week later, I found out that they snatched the line alright, but not me. I saw the new line, all 50 of them, on the yard one afternoon. I did my best to hold back the tears and not show my disappointment. I waved to the couple of girls that made the line that I had become close to these last few weeks. Carmen was one of them. She smiled at me, and waved back as inconspicuously as she could. One of the big sisters saw me, came over to me, and asked me if I was ok. She told me not to give up, and to hang in there. How considerate of her, I thought.

Bernard came over that night after work and tried to console me as best as he could. My aunt did everything she could not to say I told you so. My dad told me not to worry, and that if it was meant to be then it would be. Monica said, "Fuck them!" So, that was it. I didn't make the line even though I gave it my best.

4

SAVING ALL MY LOVE

Senior Year

Being a senior in college was a mixture of excitement, anticipation, and anxiety. Where did those four years go? What happens next? Should I go back home, should I relocate, should I stay here?

Monica kicked out her trifling and nasty roommate (her words, not mine), so I moved in with her around the middle of August. I had lived with my Aunt Max since Freshman year, so this would be the first time that I lived on my own. I couldn't wait to move in. I saved up as much money as I could from my summer job so that I could be financially comfortable my last year.

Monica and I enjoyed being roommates this last year. I studied in the evening, she studied late night/early morning. She worked, I did work study. Of course we would have some disagreements, but it was nothing that we couldn't handle or get over. We never had a lot of people over which was fine with me. We did have a couple of parties to celebrate our birthdays.

Graduation day was on Mother's Day. My whole family and a couple of close friends from home had come down to Hampton to see me walk across that stage. My mom and dad were so proud of me, you could see it written all over their faces. At that time, graduating from Pirate U was probably the most exciting thing that had ever happened to me. I was so grateful and thankful that I had made it, and was looking forward to the next phase in my life.

Well, that next phase would be graduate school. Monica moved back to Chicago after graduation. I had my own small apartment in Hampton, and worked as a graduate assistant while attending graduate school. Graduate school was no joke, and studying consumed most of my free time.

I didn't really date much over the last couple of years except for Bernard. He had me whipped, I can't deny it. At some point, he moved into his own apartment and we continued to see each other regularly. He still worked the evening shift, so we usually saw each other late after he got off work.

One date that I remember vividly was when he took me to see Phyllis Hyman at the Hampton Coliseum. I had never seen her live in concert, so I was excited. If you've ever seen her on stage, it's like she was right at home. She walked out on stage and would come right out of her shoes. Sultry, sexy, powerful, that was Phyllis.

The next couple of years zoomed by with studying, working part-time, and dating Bernard. Before I knew it, I had completed graduate school and was ready to move back home to Richmond. I was sad that he and I would be doing the long distance thing, but he assured me that we would still see each other and that nothing would change.

Returning back home after living away for six years felt a bit strange for awhile. I did the temp thing in the business office for a local hotel for a few months until I got my first real job with Panther University in their admissions department. Over the next few years, I made my career my focus. My ultimate goal was to become the president of a university somewhere, so that's where I kept that focus.

Bernard and I would take turns visiting each other. One Thanksgiving, we went to his dad's house in DC for the holiday. He surprised me one Christmas and came to my cousin's house for dinner. We basically would alternate between me going down to Hampton and him coming up to visit me in Richmond. I missed him something terrible. He had become such a part of my life, my routine when I lived in Hampton. I wasn't feeling this long distance relationship thing. "Don't put all your eggs in one basket!" my dad would always say. Basically, don't put all your everything into one person is what he meant.

Guys asked me out, and I did go out on a few dates trying to be sociable and to keep my options open. I remember I went out on date with Tammy, a close girlfriend that I grew up with, and her friend Tommy's cousin. The guys cooked out on the grill, made strawberry banana daiquiris, we went bowling, and had a really nice time talking and laughing. I could tell that Tommy's cousin was feeling me, and he even asked me out. Actually, he asked me if I wanted to take a ride with him that night on his bike. I think he thought I was supposed to be impressed or something because he had a motorcycle. He even seemed to have a bit of an attitude when I turned him down. The evening was nice and so was that bike, but I just wasn't interested. Nobody had compared to Bernard. The way he walked, talked, looked... Nobody could touch him or get me to look twice. Bernard was the one I wanted. I guess you could say I was saving all my love for him.

5

BREAK UP TO MAKE UP

After college, Monica and I kept in contact and tried to visit each other either in Richmond, Hampton, or Chicago at least once a year. She had become the business manager at her aunt's firm in downtown Chicago. She did that for many years until she eventually took over the reins of the business when her aunt retired.

Monica met this older guy a couple of years after she moved back to Chicago. They begin dating and decided to get married in 2000. I was thrilled when she asked me to be her maid of honor. I was so happy for her.

I arrived to Chicago a couple of days before the wedding. Her closest girlfriends had planned a girl's spa day the day before the wedding. She was so surprised. We all had massages, facials, manicures, and pedicures. The finest men you ever want to see did our massages. I don't know where these brothas came from, but I damn sure had not seen nobody that remotely looked that good in Richmond. The men were definitely the icing on the wedding cake!

Kyle and Monica's wedding was absolutely beautiful, and we had so much fun at the reception. It was a perfect day. I had tried to get Bernard to come to Chicago with me, but he said he couldn't get off work. Believe it or not, he and I had been dating ten years. Not sure where that time went, but being a part of Monica's wedding made me think more and more about my future with Bernard. Whenever the subject of marriage would come up, he would get nervous or change the subject. You would think the word marriage was synonymous with the word vomit because he sure would start to look faint like he was about to throw up when anybody would mention about us getting married.

Ten years is a long time to date somebody. Four out of the ten years, I was in college and graduate school. The last six were spent trying to hang on to a long distance relationship and trying to move up the university administration career ladder. I know we broke up with each other at least three if not four times.

I remember this one time when Bernard came to visit me in Richmond. We hadn't seen each other in about a month, so I couldn't wait to see him. I was so excited, I went out and bought this little sexy nightie and had planned to cook a nice dinner for us.

While I was waiting for him to arrive, my phone rang. It was Bernard. I could tell in his voice that something was wrong. He told me that we needed to talk. He said that the long distance thing wasn't working for him, and that he had met someone else. I was silent for a while because I really didn't know what to say. After I gathered myself together, I said, "I thought you said that you could handle the long distance, and I thought that you loved me. Why are you doing this now after all this time?" "Caryn, I do love you, but I am not ready to get married and the long distance is just too much." "Well how the hell can you love me if you are saying you want to be with someone else?" I replied, now in tears. "I'm not saying I want to be with someone else. I just said I met somebody that's all. I'm confused." "Well you know what, if you want to be with somebody else, then be with them. Your loss!" I said then slammed down the phone. I think I must have cried all night long. I tell you, a broken heart has got to be one of the most worst feelings in the world.

I told my mother what happened the next day. She told me to go on with my life. I never forgot her words, "He will be back, they always come back." Sure enough, Bernard called me about a week later. He said he needed to see me and asked if I would come down to visit him in Hampton. You know I went. We talked, and then our clothes fell off... That break up lasted all but maybe two weeks.

Then there was our ten year Pirate University reunion. Monica and I had been planning to attend this for months. We couldn't believe that we had been out of college for ten years. We were looking forward to the reunion and seeing old classmates. Of course, she was still talking about going to those parties. Some things never change! She and her husband were flying in from Chicago, and Bernard and I were supposed to be meeting up with them at the hotel.

I called Bernard the day before I was supposed to ride down to Hampton for the reunion, and he told me that he had other plans and couldn't make it. "It's your reunion, so you and Monica go and hang out," he said. After going back and forth on the phone, it turned into a huge argument with him telling me not to come to his place because he was not going to be there. I told him that he didn't have to ever worry about me coming to see him again. I was livid. How could he be so insensitive?

I called Monica crying and told her what happened, and she told me not to worry about his ass and that I could go to the reunion activities with her and her husband. Oh great, now I don't have a date for the damn dance. Too late of notice to try to scrounge up a back-up date. So I cancelled the hotel reservations I had made for us and decided to spend the weekend at my Aunt Max's house.

I was really hurt, but I went to the reunion and had a great time without him. I could tell a couple of guys were interested in me, and we exchanged phone numbers and e-mails so that we could keep in touch. One of my classmates even said, "You still got it going on Caryn, your man should be ashamed of himself for not being here with you." I just smiled at the compliment. He damn sure was right though. I looked too good to be here alone.

The whole time I was in Hampton that weekend, I wasn't tempted not even once to go by Bernard's apartment or to call him. I just knew this time it was over because I had no desire to call or see him. About a month or so later, I agreed to go out to dinner with a guy I met at church. Yes, church. His name was Michael. He was the business manager at my church, single, and was always nice to me. Not really my type, but it wasn't like I was trying to marry him or anything. Just something to do.

Michael said he would pick me up Saturday around 7:00. I figured he was probably an on-time and prompt kind of guy, if there is such a thing, because he just seemed like the type. So, I was dressed and ready by 6:30.

I realized that I needed to get something out of my car, so I opened my apartment door and to my surprise Bernard was standing there. Now, it's 6:35 right about now and I am expecting Michael any minute. "Hello Caryn," he said in that sexy voice of his. Ok, so now what do I do? Part of me wants to slap him, and the other part of me wants to take his pants off and straddle him. So, I take a deep breath and say, "What are you doing here Bernard?" "I miss you Caryn. You still love me?" Although my knees were buckling, I was able to get the words out and say, "I have plans right now, so this is not a good time; just like you did a month ago when you reneged on taking me to my 10 year reunion." "I deserve that and I ain't mad, but it's not over Caryn. I have been trying to reach you for a month, and you have not returned none of my calls. I'm here now and we need to settle this. You go ahead with your plans for the evening, and I'll be here when you get back," he responded with a smirk. Now I'm thinking what in the world? Is he going to trip when Michael gets here? Do I send Michael home, do I send Bernard home, do I get the hell out and leave them both here?

I tried to call Michael on his cell, but by this time he was now pulling up to my apartment. I told him that something had come up unexpectedly and apologized as best as I could. He seemed to be cool with it and told me to call him if I needed him. What I nice guy, I thought.

I braced myself and went back into my apartment to "settle this." "So, talk," I said. "Let's get married

Caryn. Me and you baby, let's do it." "Bernard, please. Are you serious? Why now all of a sudden?" "Caryn, I've missed you these last few weeks, and I don't want to lose you." He pulled out a ring from his pocket and placed it on my finger. "This was my mom's. I love you and you know that."

Bernard and I talked for I know a couple of hours, and ended up having pizza delivered. After we ate, we talked some more and I told him that I would marry him. We decided that we would live together while we were making plans to get married and agreed to start looking for a house the following weekend.

The best thing about breaking up is making up. There is just something about make-up sex. The sex is intense, passionate, and just freaking hot. Bernard carried me into my bedroom and laid me down on the bed. He pulled my blouse off and started with my breasts. He had a way of caressing my whole body and when he finally touched me there, his hands sent me to another place. I couldn't wait for Bernard to make love to me. I reached ecstasy with him over and over again that night. Break up to make up. Whew!

By that fall, Bernard and I had found a house in the Hampton area. I was happy to be back in Tidewater and close to Pirate U. We were excited about our house and starting our lives together. We decided not to go anywhere for Christmas that year and to spend it together for the first time in our new home. I couldn't believe that it was finally happening. We were together, and planning to get married! I was so happy and ready. God knows I was ready.

6

NOTHING GOING ON BUT THE RENT

I moved from Richmond that November, but kept my job at the university. I found a commuter vanpool that left from Hampton at 6:45 am every morning, so I officially became a commuter. By this time I had been working at Panther University about eight years or so and had worked my way up to the position of Assistant Director of Admissions. It was worth the commute to get to my ultimate career goal of becoming a university president. I had to alternate though between driving myself and taking the vanpool due to the demands of my new role at work.

The last couple of years Bernard had been working the 7:00 am to 3:00 pm shift which he loved after all those years of working the 3:00pm to 12:00am shift. My day started pretty early with my meeting the vanpool every morning by 6:40, riding an hour and 10 minutes to Richmond, working all day, riding the van back to Hampton, getting back by 6:15 in the evening. Most of the time I cooked, but every once and awhile Bernard would cook too. My aunt told me to cook at least two meals on Sunday which would last us through the week. It made sense and I had every intention of doing that at some point, but I just hadn't quite got into that routine just yet. I mean who wants to spend the whole weekend cooking?

I had been used to cooking for one, numero uno. A meal that would have stretched three days for me lasted one day for the two of us. Cooking for a man felt like feeding an army. He ate, and ate, and ate. Needless to say, I had to change the way I bought groceries and the way I prepared meals.

The first few months were great. I was still getting into the routine of commuting, and Bernard and I were adjusting to living together and all that comes with it. We decided to get married in October and planned a destination wedding in St. Thomas, Virgin Islands.

Around the middle of May, Bernard came home one day and told me that he had been laid off from his job indefinitely. They told him they would contact him once they had more work or something like that. I told him that we would be ok, and that we were in this for better or worse. He responded, "More like for richer or poorer." I could tell that he was upset and worried, but I tried to be upbeat and encouraging. We now had a mortgage, household bills, personal bills, and he had a car note to pay. Bernard changed his clothes and told me that he needed to go out for awhile and would be back. He came back that night pretty late. He smelled like he had fallen into a lake of gin and vodka.

By July, his company still had not called him back to work. There's just nothing worse than an unemployed man. His confidence, self-worth, everything is just shot to shit. No matter what I did or said, nothing could console Bernard or make him feel better about himself or the situation. He started to spend more time away from home. When he would finally come home, it was usually pretty late, and he would reek of alcohol. He used the little bit of money that he got from unemployment for his car note and his personal bills. I was doing my best to maintain the household on my income, but it was rough. It seemed like the more I did, the more Bernard resented me.

In the midst of everything, his stepmother called him and told him that his dad had been arrested for a DUI. He'd been in a small accident, but was ok. "Crazy ass old man! What in the hell was he thinking?" he said.

I always thought Bernard's relationship with his family was rather odd and off and on again. Well, this new development with his dad just added more fuel to his already burning flame.

We had been planning to have an engagement party around the middle of July. I had really been looking forward to our family and friends celebrating with us. I must say that Bernard's being laid off threw a big old monkey wrench in our plans and especially our budget. The week before the party, Bernard was moping around acting like he was uninterested about the fact that our backyard was jacked up and that there were still a few things that needed to be done around the house. The reality that we were expecting over forty guests in a week didn't seem to faze him. I, on the other hand, was getting a bit worried that these folks were going to show up and would know that something was terribly wrong. Bernard didn't want anyone, other than our parents, to know that he'd been laid off. So on top of everything, I had to put on a front.

Well, he came through at the last minute. The day before the party, he mowed, trimmed, clipped, and whatever the hell else he needed to do to get the backyard straight. He also took care of the minor repairs that needed to be done in the house.

By the time the guests started to arrive the next day, he seemed to be back to his old self.

Friends and family came from all over. Monica and her husband came in from Chicago. It was good to see her. We didn't get a chance to really catch up, but just her being there meant a lot. Everyone seemed to have a good time and enjoyed themselves. My Aunt Max catered the party, and everybody talked about how good the food was. She is the best cook! Ribs, homemade cole slaw, potato salad, tossed salad, bbq chicken, scallops wrapped in bacon, cakes, pies. Yum! I'm getting hungry now just thinking about it. We had so much food leftover that folks took plates home, and we had enough to last us a few days too. My girlfriend Tammy and my mom spent the night with us. The rest of the guests either drove back home or stayed in a nearby hotel.

After breakfast, Tammy and my mom got on the road and headed back home to Richmond. I was a little tired from yesterday but felt good. I felt like everything was going to be ok. Unfortunately that feeling didn't last long. After Tammy and my mom left, Bernard said he was going out. When he finally came back home, I could tell that he had been drinking.

While all of this was going on, I was still commuting every day to Richmond and trying to finalize the plans for our destination wedding. My outlet was my career. I loved working with young people and working in a college setting especially an HBCU. I had started taking a course towards my doctorate, and had asked my director at the time to mentor me for the next level. I worked hard to prove myself and focused on work while I was in Richmond, not what was going on at home. When I got home though, it was a different story. Bernard was out all of the time, and when he was home, he would be moody and irritable. I was beginning to be more alone than with him. Luckily, my Aunt Max was nearby, so she was my voice of reason and my vent partner.

One Saturday afternoon, I convinced Bernard to go for a ride. It was pretty hot that day, but I felt like we both needed to get out and just spend some time together. We really had not done much of anything since he'd been laid off. As we were driving, Bernard spotted a sports utility vehicle with a for sale sign parked in the front lot of a car dealership. We decided to check it out. He had been talking about wanting an SUV for a while. This was definitely a nice one, and seemed to be reasonably priced. So, we went for a test drive. Why in the world did we do that? Once we took that ride, Bernard was pretty much sold. The fact that he had been having problems with his own car didn't help much.

After we got out of the truck he said, "So Caryn baby can we get it?" "Can we get it, are you serious, Bernard?" "Look, we can trade my car in for the down payment. You know my credit ain't that good right now, and I'm not working. The money that I was using to pay my car note, I'll just give to you to go towards the truck each month. But that's up to you," he said. I could tell that he really wanted it, and it wouldn't break the bank. Part of me wanted him to just feel better, and I really did like the truck too. So I said, "Ok, where do I sign?"

Completing the paperwork seemed like it took forever. Bernard cleaned out everything in his car, and turned his keys over to the salesman. When the spotless, clean, shiny truck pulled up, we both looked at each other and grinned. When we got home, he made love to me and held me in his arms the rest of that night. Maybe now things won't be so strained around here I thought. The next day, he went over to a friend's house to show off the truck. He was gone from early that afternoon to 9:00 that night. When he got back, he smelled like smoke and liquor.

A couple of weeks later, I came home one evening from work and had decided to cook one of Bernard's favorite meals. I hoped that it would pick up his spirits some, and keep his butt at home too. I got home around 6:30. I quickly changed clothes and went right to the kitchen. I did crab cakes, baked potatoes, and green beans. By 8:00, he hadn't gotten home and I couldn't reach him on his cell phone. By 8:45, I was so mad that I barely ate myself and went up to bed. Midnight, 2:00 am, 3:00 am, still no Bernard. He still hadn't called me, and his cell phone was going straight into voice-mail.

The house alarm went off at 5:30 am. Bernard walked into the bedroom. He looked a hot mess and the stench of alcohol was oozing from his pores. I had not slept at all that night. I just knew he was hurt or dead in a ditch somewhere. He looked at me and said, "Go head Caryn, go head and say it. I already know what you are going to say. Just so you know, I went to the club, had too many drinks and couldn't make it back home. I stayed on Jay's couch." I looked at him and said, "Bernard, you need to get your drunk ass together. I did not sign up for this bull shit and can't deal with it no more. We can't get married like this. For the record, I'm not as stupid as you think I am." "But Caryn I never said you were stupid," he responded. He went downstairs to the living room and just sat in the chair in a daze. I got dressed, grabbed my lunch, and headed to catch that damn vanpool.

The next few weeks were better. His company called him back mid-August. Talking about a relief. J-O-B! A month and a half before the wedding, he went back to work. This time though he was now on the 11:00 pm to 7:00 am shift. I was a bit disappointed in the new shift, but at least he was working and this house could finally get back to normal.

Towards the middle of September, hurricane Isabel hit the East Coast. Electricity was out from Richmond down to the Hampton area. We were without power for about a week and a half. Since Bernard was now working the night shift, I was pretty much fending for myself the whole time the power was out after that storm. No television, no radio, no lights, no nothing for almost two weeks.

Actually, I felt like I had been fending for myself this whole summer. Trying to maintain all of the household expenses, enduring Bernard's "ain't got no job" drama, and then dealing with the storm's aftermath alone was a bit much. Then there was the nagging in the back of my mind about our upcoming wedding. Bernard said he was ready to make this step, but was he?

7

STRAIGHT FROM THE HEART

Two weeks before the wedding, I asked Bernard if he sure he was ready to get married. He looked at me and asked me why was I asking him that. "Bernard, the way you've been acting over the last few months has not been that of someone who is ready to be a married man." He responded, "Caryn, if I told you that I wanted to wait awhile longer, would you leave me?" "Yes, I would, I'd have to. We've been together for thirteen years, long enough for you to know. That's not the reason you should marry me though. Marry me because you want to, not for the fear of losing me." He didn't say anything, he just had that damn look like he was going to throw up. He finally said, "It's been me and you all this time, and you know I love you Caryn. I could always count on you even when I couldn't even count on my own family. You have always been here for me even when I didn't deserve it. I'm ready. When do we leave for the islands, man, irie?" "Are you sure Bernard, are you really sure?" "Yes, Caryn. Straight from the heart baby, straight from the heart."

That October we left for St. Thomas, Virgin Islands. Tammy was my maid of honor, and Jay was Bernard's best man. Our parents were with us too of course. Monica wanted to come, but she was pregnant and expecting her twins. Although it was early in her pregnancy, she was having complications and didn't want to take any chances.

We arrived on the island on a Friday afternoon just in time to pick up the marriage license from the courthouse. My mother and Aunt Max were with us, but everyone else flew in at separate times. My wedding planner Lena greeted us when we checked in. We met with her to go over the details, but for the most part she had everything already taken care of. All we had to do was show up the next day.

The resort was absolutely beautiful. The grounds were sculptured and neatly manicured with flowers and coconut palm trees almost around every corner. The view from our room was breathtaking. The ocean was so clear. All you could see was aqua bluish green for miles. Our balcony had a couple of lounging chairs and a nice sized table. Bernard was already figuring out how he could get me on that balcony that night.

Our wedding guests met us for dinner that evening at the resort's main restaurant. All of the meals at the resort were mouth watering, absolutely delicious. They mainly had seafood such as conch, lobster, and freshly caught fish. The native dishes like the stews and curries, such as island-style mutton, curried chicken, and conch and the fried plantains were standard. Bernard and Jay got hooked on the ginger beer.

After dinner, our parents turned in for the evening. Bernard, Jay, Tammy, and I decided to go to the club located at the resort. They had a live local Caribbean band. We mostly listened to the music, but we did dance some. I could tell Jay and Tammy were feeling each other. Not sure if it was truly attraction or more of the ginger beer and just being cut up in the romance of the island. After awhile, they left us and went off to walk the beach.

Bernard and I left the club soon after and went up to our room. We sat on the balcony for a good while just enjoying the ocean breeze. We were really tired because we had a long day with traveling and everything. Tomorrow was the big day. Seems like as soon as we closed our eyes, daylight was coming through the balcony blinds. He reached for my hand and said, "Good morning, this is it. Are you ready to be Mrs. Bernard Williams?" Before I could respond,

I could feel his hand massaging my inner thigh and gradually moving upwards. "No, Bernard, not now! We gotta wait until after the wedding." "I want to remind you of the real reason why you want to be Mrs. Williams," he said as he continued to fondle me between my legs. As much as I wanted to stay in bed with him until it was time to jump the broom, I rolled out of the bed and went into the bathroom and started to get dressed. He tried to pout, but I reminded him that we were meeting everyone for breakfast and then my mom, Tammy, Aunt Max and I had massages scheduled at the resort spa afterwards. "We have a lifetime of making love," I told him.

We all met for breakfast around 10:00 or so. I didn't ask any questions, but Tammy and Jay came in together and looked a bit too cozy. She walked by me and whispered, "Yes I slept with him, and will do it again the next chance I get." All I could do was smile.

The breakfast was buffet style, but they did have omelets cooked to order. For the most part, we talked about the wedding schedule for the day like arrival times, dinner, and how good the food was. I heard Jay asked Bernard if he was all set. Bernard grabbed my hand, looked at me, smiled, and said "most definitely."

After breakfast, everyone kind of went their separate ways. Aunt Max, Tammy, my mom, and I headed for the spa. When we arrived, the aroma of eucalyptus mint and lavender almost immediately relaxed us. I couldn't wait for my hot stone massage. The massage therapist suggested that we have our massages out on the beach. As wonderful as that sounded, I had to pass. My hair had already started to fall due to the humidity, and I didn't want to do anything that would jack it up. We all enjoyed our massages and the royal treatment. They served us flavored herbal teas, macadamia nuts, and the best orange pumpkin bread. They pampered us so much that we had to drag ourselves out of there so we could start getting ready for the wedding.

We went back to my room to get dressed. Bernard was in Jay's room and was getting dressed there. Up until now, it really hadn't hit me that we were here on this beautiful tropical island and I was getting ready to marry the man that I have loved since I was 20 years old. I guess I had gotten so caught up on the travel arrangements, getting here, and making sure everyone else got here that I hadn't had time to let it sink in. As I stood on the balcony and looked out over the ocean, feelings of joy and anticipation started to overwhelm me. I am marrying Bernard, I am marrying Bernard.

My dad came by my room to give me his daddy's girl speech. I told him how much I loved him, how much I respected him, and how he has always been and will always be my first love. Even though he and my mom divorced when I was a little girl, we had always been close and his being here today meant the world to me. When he left, my mom kind of rolled her eyes, but I wasn't even about to deal with that today of all days. Whatever issues they had were theirs, not mine.

My mom was never really one for a lot of words but she showed her support by helping me get dressed and making sure I had everything I needed. Tammy's role was to keep tabs on Bernard and Jay to make sure Bernard didn't get cold feet and try to chicken out at the last minute. Bernard's dad called me around this time and assured me that Bernard wasn't going anywhere and that he was in this for the long haul.

At 3:45, Lena, the wedding planner, arrived at my hotel room to pick me up to take us over to the gazebo where the wedding would be taking place at 4:00. "Caryn, how beautiful you look. What a pretty lady! Are you all ready to go?" she said with her island accent. "In about five minutes," I said as I was still trying to get my hair in place. "Ok girl, this is it. I am so happy for you. You and Bernard deserve today after all ya'll have been through over the years," Tammy said as a tear fell down her face.

Tammy and I had been friends since kinder-garten. We have always been close and had a special bond. She had been divorced for a couple of years, but wasn't bitter about marriage at all. She embraced the opportunity to marry again.

"And don't forget to throw that damn bouquet my way!" Tammy said as she went out the door. My mom just looked at me and said, "You are the one best thing that I ever did in my life and I know I don't tell you often, but I love you." Ok, so now we're both tearing up, and I'm like I can't mess up my makeup yet!

We piled in some kind of cart thing that Lena was driving and headed to the wedding location. Once we got to the main lobby, Lena had a photographer and videographer there waiting for us. After we took a series of pictures, we proceeded up to the top of the hotel which had a door that lead to the outside kind of like on the roof. When I got to the top of the stairs, my dad was waiting there for me. Lena opened the door, and Tammy went out first. The gazebo was decorated with all shades of beautiful hibiscus flowers, and the scenic Caribbean backdrop was just breathtaking. Then it was our turn. My dad escorted me towards the gazebo. I could see Bernard standing there next to the preacher just grinning and watching me as I walked down the aisle leading up to the gazebo. He looked so handsome standing there tall with his ivory linen suit.

We'd decided that we wanted our wedding attire to be comfortable and suitable for the weather and the whole island experience. Bernard wanted linen, so he picked out a nice ivory two piece with a short sleeve shirt and slacks. My dress was long and flowing, form fitting, low cut in the front with the back out, with a small train. Not too formal, but just right for a beach wedding; more like classy sexy.

Even though it wasn't a long distance to walk, it seemed like it took us forever to get to the gazebo. At one point, my dad said, "You know I'm not doing this again." "Me either," I replied with us both trying not to laugh. Bernard reached for my hand when we finally reached the entrance of the gazebo. The afternoon was perfect. As we stood there, we could feel the cross breeze from the ocean behind us. I didn't know what to expect, but the ceremony was pretty traditional, and the preacher with his St. Thomas accent had some very encouraging and powerful words for us. He even referenced from the bible I Corinthians 13: 4-6: "Love is patient and kind. Love is not jealous or boastful or proud or rude. It does not demand its own way. It is not irritable, and it keeps no record of being wronged. It does not rejoice about injustice but rejoices whenever the truth wins out. Love never gives up, never loses faith, is always hopeful, and endures through every circumstance."

"I now pronounce you husband and wife. Bernard, you may kiss your lovely bride Caryn." Those were the magic words. Every girl's dream. Bernard kissed me, and told me he loved me. Everyone clapped and started coming up to us with hugs, kisses, and well wishes.

After we all finished taking pictures, we did the champagne toasts and cut the cake. The cake was delicious. It was tiered, decorated with flowers with lemon frosting and a raspberry filling. I must say

I was very pleased with how well the St. Thomas' wedding planning staff coordinated everything from our arrival up to the ceremony itself. Everything was meticulously done with their native flare. I couldn't have asked for a more beautiful place to marry the man I loved.

We had dinner in the main restaurant. Everybody from the staff to the guests kept telling me how beautiful my dress was and how good Bernard and I looked together. Dinner was scrumptious just as all of the meals had been so far. Aunt Max and my mom both made a comment that Bernard had not stopped drinking since we had the champagne at the wedding. Bernard was one who could definitely hold his liquor so it wasn't like his balance would be off or he would be pissy stinky drunk. He would just be a weird sort of calm and you could smell alcohol coming from his pores. That's how he was by the time we got back to our room. He fell straight across the bed with his clothes on.

I took of my wedding dress and went on in the bathroom to freshen up. About fifteen minutes later, I came out with a sexy, white lingerie that my Aunt Max had given me for our wedding night. Bernard was knocked out. He had taken his clothes off and gotten in the bed, but he was sleeping hard, snoring and everything. I called his name a couple of times, but couldn't get him to wake up. I was a bit disappointed, but I was tired too. I got on in the bed, and he immediately I guess out of reflex put his arms around me. The smell of alcohol was so strong, I had to turn my back to him.

Bernard woke up early the next morning saying, "Good morning Mrs. Williams, wake up." I guess he realized that he missed my entrance last night because he had that look like he wanted to devour me. Or perhaps that was his hangover look. "Is this what I have to look forward to until death do us part? You always gonna look this sexy?" he said now tickling me. He picked up the blanket with me in it, and led me to the balcony. We made love for the first time as husband and wife as the sun rose over the island.

Our guests all went back home on Sunday. Bernard and I stayed another night. Sunday, after breakfast we were back and forth between the beach and the pool. We did go into town for dinner for our last night. After we got back to the hotel, we sat out on the beach talking under the stars into the wee hours of the morning. Before we went to bed, Bernard pulled me to him close and said, "I think I'm gonna like this marriage thang. Now take them clothes off."

Our last day in St. Thomas was just perfect. When it was time for us to leave that next afternoon, I really wasn't ready to go. "I wish we could just live here Bernard," I said as he was checking us out the hotel. "We'll have to come back for our one year anniversary, how about that?" he replied slapping me on my butt. Lena met us as we were checking out and gave us some of our wedding photos and DVD. She kissed us both goodbye and said with her native slang, "All right my brotha and sistah, be happy and be blessed."

We had a pretty good flight from St. Thomas to Atlanta. We slept most of the way. When we arrived in Atlanta's airport, we had about a forty minute layover. Since we had to wait, I decided to call home and listen to our messages. "Bernard, can you believe we have nine messages?" "Caryn, why don't you relax, I'll check the messages." He reached for the phone, but then he stopped when he saw my face. Message 1: "Don't marry him; you need to call me"; Message 2: "Bitch you better call me"; Message 3: "You think you all that because you married Bernard? He ain't nothing but a lying ass. You don't know him like you think you do. What you need to know is who he's been fucking the last four years." Message 4: "Hey little girl, this is Grandma. I just wanted to congratulate you and Bernard. Love you." The rest of the messages were hang-ups.

The phone fell out of my hand, but Bernard caught it before it hit the ground. I started to feel nauseous, and my mouth started watering. I ran into the restroom and barely made it to the stall before I threw up. I kept hearing "last call for flight 3445 to Richmond, last call for flight 3445 to Richmond" in the background. I wiped my face and pulled myself together and walked out of the bathroom. Bernard was standing there waiting for me. I assumed he must have checked the voice-mail messages too now by the way he was acting and the look he had on his face. We didn't have time to say a word though because we had to run and catch our flight.

Once we got settled on the plane, Bernard grabbed my hand and said, "Caryn, baby this is not as bad as it looks. I mean it's crazy as hell, but just let me explain. Missy..." I stopped him and said, "Missy, who the hell is Missy?" "Missy is a friend that I met a couple of years ago back when you and I had broken up. We've still been kind of cool, and have kept in contact. Just friends though. But when she found out I was getting married, she kind of lost it." "This doesn't make any sense Bernard. If you all are just friends, then why would she give a damn if you are getting married to the point that she's leaving these crazy ass messages before our wedding?" "Caryn, believe me. She don't mean nothing, nothing too me. She's just jealous because I never wanted to be with her. You know me, I wouldn't have married you if there was someone else," he said.

I had more questions but it was obvious that being on this plane was not the right time to talk about this. When we landed in Richmond, we got in the truck and drove down to Hampton. I was so confused that I really didn't know what to say. I mean I knew that the conversation was nowhere near over but I was just so perplexed about the whole thing. Bernard must could read my angst because he said, "Are you ok? Sweetheart, don't let this ruin our honeymoon. Believe me, this is nothing." "Bernard, so you are telling me that this Missy or whoever the hell she is, is somebody from your past and that's it?" "Caryn, I swear on my momma's grave." "How did she get our phone number?" "I don't know, the phone book maybe." "When was the last time you talked to her?" "I don't know maybe a couple of months ago."

This went on for the whole hour and a half drive home. Every time I asked him a question, he had a plausible answer. When we got home, I told him that this whole thing was bizarre and that I didn't know what to believe. He said, raising his voice a little bit, "Look Caryn, I have answered all of your questions. Do you fucking trust me or what?" I just looked at him. I went on up to bathroom and sat there on the floor for a few minutes in a daze. After awhile I finally took my clothes off and stepped into the shower. The tone of his voice and the gall of that question and the whole situation was just too much. I couldn't hold it in anymore. The tears started to fall, and I cried like a baby. "Oh my God, oh my God," I screamed as the water fell down my body. Bernard ran into the bathroom and grabbed me. "Caryn, I am so sorry baby, I am so sorry. I didn't mean to hurt you. I shouldn't have raised my voice. This shit has upset me too because you're hurt and upset. Look at me, look at me Caryn. Stop crying. He's wiping my tears with tissues at this point. I love you. I married you. I wouldn't hurt you, I'd never hurt you." He gently washed my body and dried me off. He picked me up and took me into our bedroom. He laid me down, passionately started kissing me. He kissed my nipples, my stomach, and then he went lower. I felt his lips and he looked up at me with a fire, a fierceness that I had not seen in years. And then I felt him. It was like an indescribable heat. My body responded with pleasure.

The next morning, Bernard cooked breakfast while I unpacked our suitcases. I felt a little better this morning after our talk and after last night. Bernard yelled from the kitchen, "Ok Caryn after we eat I want some more of your good stuff from last night." I smiled. Before I went downstairs to breakfast, I realized that I had forgotten to change my work voice-mail to indicate that I will be out of the office for the next week. When I called my voice-mail, I decided to go ahead and check the messages so I wouldn't have as many when I returned back to work the following week.

The first message was my director wishing me and Bernard wedding wishes, the second message was from another co-worker, "Hey girl, I just wanted to tell you that I am happy for you; jealous as hell but happy!" "Breakfast is ready," I could hear Bernard yelling from downstairs. I figured I would listen to this last message because my stomach was growling something terrible. I had worked up a hell of an appetite from last night. "Caryn, my name is Missy. I don't know what you have heard, but I wanted you to hear the truth from me. Bernard and I have been together and have been in love for almost four years. We even had a baby boy together that we lost. The last time we were together was last Thursday, the night before you left for your wedding. He has been lying to you for years, and knowing him like I do, he's probably lying to you now. I am mad as hell because he told me that he was going to call the wedding off. I am not some crazy woman trying to get back at him. Bernard told me Thursday night that he loved me and would always love me."

Before she could finish someone else took the phone and said, "Fuck that bitch. Everybody knows that he don't want her ass no way. He just married her because he was pissed at you. Yeah, bitch we got something for yo ass." I could hear in the background that other person saying, "You need to fuck Mrs. So called Williams up." Then I heard the phone go silent.

8

LIVING IN CONFUSION

I sat on the bed confused trying to figure out my next move. I didn't have long though to figure things out because I could hear Bernard coming up the stairs. He took one look at me and said, "Oh Lord, what now?" I handed him the phone, dialed my work voice-mail, and replayed the messages. When he hung up the phone, he looked down and then away from me. I calmly said, "Bernard, I need you to be honest with me. This woman not only tried to stop our wedding, but then feels as if she has the fucking right to call my job to talk to me. On top of that, she has people threatening me on the phone. Is it true? The relationship, the baby, all of it. Is it true? One tear and then more tears start to fall down his cheek, but he's still silent. If you ever loved me, tell me the truth!"

I started to get a slight headache as feelings of rage and anger welled up like boiling water inside of me. "Yes, Caryn it's true. All of it. The baby was a miscarriage, and I don't even know if it was mine. But it's over, I swear to you. I told her last Thursday that we couldn't be together, and that I wanted to be with and marry you. She's mad at me, not you. She can't let it go. She just can't let it go." "Do you love her?" I asked. He looked at me with a look of defeat. He fell down on his knees, tears still falling, but didn't say anything. "Do you love her, I yelled?" "What do you want me to say, Caryn? I just looked at him dead in his eyes. Ok, yes I love her. But I chose you." "You lied to me for years, you lied to me last night, you lied to me on our wedding day. How could you do this to me Bernard?"

Now tears are falling down my face and I feel like I just got hit by a speeding mack truck. Bernard in a frantic started begging me, "Please believe me Caryn. I will do whatever you want, believe me baby please believe me. I love you. I need you, not her. Ok, I fucked up, I lied two weeks ago, last month, last year, the year before that. But when I said I do, til death do us part on Saturday on that island, I meant it with all of my heart. Straight from the heart." His cell phone started to ring. He didn't answer it, but the person kept calling. "Is that her?" "Yes. I was trying to avoid her, but she's not giving up. I need to handle this." The phone rang for the fourth time, and this time he answered. "Calm down, calm down. Baby, please don't cry. This has got to stop. Ok, I will be over there," I heard him saying on the phone.

Listening to him console this Missy was a bit much. I left him on the floor, and went downstairs. My head was spinning. The aroma of sausage was still in the air from the breakfast that we never ate. I went into the kitchen and there was sausage, eggs, fried potatoes, and biscuits on the stove. Bernard had cooked this wonderful breakfast. It was supposed to be our first home cooked breakfast at our home as a married couple; it was supposed to be a perfect day just making love and being in love; it wasn't supposed to be like this. We had been married for three days and everything changed just like that.

Now our home phone starts ringing. The answering machine picks up, and we could hear somebody's voice: "Dammit, Bernard you're going to make me come over there and fuck your new bride up if you don't bring your ass over here, you know me. I ain't playing." Bernard had come downstairs at this point. "Bernard, now who the hell is that threatening me? Who are these people, and what kind of people do you deal with?" "That's just her sister. She'll calm down. She knows not to do anything to you, or she'll have to deal with me. I'm going over there now so I can get this shit straight."

He looked me in my eye and said, "Caryn, I know this is the worst thing that could happen. I can only imagine how you feel about me. What I can tell you is that it's over with Missy. It was over when we got off that plane." "It should have been over when you gave me that ring, your momma's ring, a year and a half ago. It should have been over all these years that I thought it was just me and you; it should have been over a long fucking time ago. Really, it never should have started. You've been sleeping with both of us for years, and I don't know who the hell she's been sleeping with. You put me in danger!" I screamed. "Tell me what to do. How can I fix it?" "I don't know, maybe we need counseling I mean I don't know. I don't even know why we are having this fucking conversation three days after our wedding," I responded. "Ok then let's set up an appointment for counseling. I'll do anything," he said.

He kissed me and said he'd be back. "I'm sorry Caryn, I don't know what else to say", and then he left. Still somewhat in shock, I looked up my employee assistance program number and set up an appointment with a counselor the following week. How embarrassing. Here we are asking for help, and have only been married about 2 minutes. I then called my gynecologist and was able to squeeze in an appointment for STDs and an HIV test for next week too. I had to make sure that I was ok and hadn't caught anything from these idiots. This was all still my first week of being married. "God help me, God, please help me."

As soon as Bernard left, the phone rung again. Although hesitant, I answered it. That same voice called me a bitch and hung up. I sat there thinking, what in the world has he gotten me into? Confusion, drama. Should I call somebody? Who could I tell? I'm supposed to be enjoying my honeymoon, but I'm sitting here while he is over at his ex girlfriend's house. What do I do?

I decided to go over my Aunt Max's house. I knew that she would be home by now since this was her early day. I called her and she told me she'd be home by 3:00. When I walked in the door, she hugged me and told me how proud and how happy she was for me. "Tell me all about the rest of the trip after we left!" she said. I proceeded to tell her what happened from the time they all left St. Thomas until the day Bernard and I left. "Oh Caryn, it sounds wonderful, romantic!" I then continued with my story, her facial expression changed, my voice started to crack, and then by the time I told her about today, she was holding me in her arms.

"Do you believe him?" "I don't know what to believe Aunt Max. He sounds sincere and he looks just as hurt as I feel." "Well counseling is definitely a start. I am so sorry baby, my goodness. And you damn sure are doing the right thing about getting tested. You can never be too careful. I know you love him, but just keep your eyes open from now on, you hear me?" At that moment, my cell phone rang. It was Bernard. "Ah huh," I answered. "I'm home Caryn, where are you?" "At Aunt Max's, I'll be home later," I said and hung up. Going to see my aunt and talking to her was good for me and what I needed. I had to tell somebody before I exploded or snapped.

When I got back home, Bernard was playing his Sony play station. The first thing he said was, "I talked to Missy and her sister. We won't be hearing from them no more. Guess what? You know I have to work this weekend. The surprise is that they put me back on the day shift." "Oh ok. You know you need to take off or get off early next Thursday because we have our appointment with the marriage counselor," was all I could muster to say. I felt drained and still somewhat confused about the whole situation. I went right upstairs and got in the bed. I didn't cook, nor did I eat. I wasn't sure, nor did I care what Bernard ate, so he was on his own that night.

The rest of the week was rather strained between us. I could tell that Bernard was trying to make me feel better about things, and I tried to not be in a funk. I wasn't myself though and I knew he could tell. We really didn't talk to anybody that week other than his dad. Bernard told his dad what happened, and his dad talked to the both of us. He basically said that we needed to put this behind us and move on with our new lives together.

"That was the past, and we needed to focus on our future," he told us.

Bernard went back to work Saturday morning, our one week anniversary. He called me a couple of times during the day to check on me. "I love you Caryn," he said. I cooked a pretty big meal by the time he got home that evening. I could tell he was surprised. Sunday he left for work at 6:45 am. As I did most Sundays, I went to church and breakfast with Aunt Max. I really needed to be in church that Sunday; I needed to pray in His sanctuary. When the soloist broke out singing "I love the Lord; He heard my cry, and pitied every groan..." my heart sank.

I spent the rest of the evening dozing on and off and watching Lifetime channel movies. Since we had leftovers from yesterday's dinner, I didn't cook. Bernard called me after work and told me that some of the guys from work where taking him out to celebrate his getting married. After I ate dinner, I went on upstairs and got ready for bed and tried to mentally get prepared for work tomorrow. Bernard got home around 10:00 that night. He took a shower, got in the bed, put his arms around me and asked, "You still love me?" He said he and some of the guys from work had gone to a bar for a few drinks and to watch the game.

When I got to work in Richmond Monday morning, I checked my voice mail praying that I didn't have anymore surprise messages. I had a couple of hang-ups from the weekend but the numbers were blocked. I knew who they were from, but tried not to let myself go there. Fortunately, I was greeted by a full calendar. The good thing is that I had enough to keep me busy and my mind occupied. Coming to Richmond was still my escape. Thank goodness I loved my job.

Wednesday evening, Bernard got home around 8:00. He said he had worked late and then went over Jay's. He must had been to the liquor store too because he took a bottle out of a brown paper bag. He opened up the bottle, I guess it was scotch, and poured himself a drink before he could even take his work clothes off.

"You know we have our appointment tomorrow at 4:00 with the marriage counselor," I reminded him. "Ok," he said and sat down and started playing video games. He didn't come to bed until after 1:00 am. That next morning, we both got up and got ready for work. Bernard says, "Caryn, I'm not going to see no counselor. We'll be ok. Missy is out of the picture. We don't need nobody all up in our business." I could feel my temperature rising. I responded, "But you said that we, that you, that you would do anything I wanted. What are we supposed to do? We need to talk to somebody…" He cut me off and said, "I am not going Caryn. It's over with her. My focus is getting us back on track. I don't need no shrink for that." On that note, he left. I cancelled the appointment when I got to work.

One thing I didn't cancel was my doctor's appointment. Friday, I went to see my gynecologist. It was rather difficult trying to explain to her why I felt that I needed these tests, but I knew that it needed to be done. I basically said, "Ok so we got married, then I found out that he'd been with someone else. Now I need to make sure that they haven't given me something that I need an antibiotic for or something than can like kill me." My doctor was very understanding, told me not to be ashamed, and that if I needed counseling, she could suggest someone for me.

I could not wait for the weekend. I just wanted not to be around anyone and crawl up in the bed. Bernard had to work again this weekend, so I'd have some time to myself. We'd officially been married for two weeks and hadn't made love since before everything went down with Missy and her sister. He'd been cautious with me. I could tell he was feeling me out, but I just couldn't, I just couldn't.

When I got home Friday evening, Bernard had fried fish, baked potatoes, and corn. I was surprised actually. I figured he would be home late, so I'd planned to come home and eat a ham sandwich and chips. I looked up on the mantel and saw that he had framed and put our wedding picture up. I saw the rest of the pictures in an envelope on the table with a note from Lena, our wedding coordinator in St. Thomas that said, "Best wishes to my lovely couple again. I wanted to get these to you soon so you can share with your loved ones. Be happy and in love."

Tears came to my eyes looking at those photos. After all that had happened after we left the island, I had almost forgotten how happy we were there and how beautiful our wedding was. Bernard didn't say anything, he just smiled and told me that dinner was ready.

Something about a man cooking dinner when you least expect it, looking sexy in his boxer shorts, reminiscing about your wedding, and just being fucking stressed out over some bull shit ex girlfriend drama changed our two week drought that night. I needed Bernard, my Bernard that night. We made love and he took me to that place over and over again.

After about the first month or so we had pretty much tried to get back into the routine of things and get back to normal and put the past of Missy behind us. My test results came back negative thank goodness. One Friday evening, I came home from work and called Bernard on his cell phone. I wanted to go to a movie, so I left him a message to call me. I laid on the couch and went through the mail. The cell phone bill had doubled, and I was like what in the world? As I looked more closely, I saw where Bernard had been calling Missy's number at all hours of the day and night and sometimes four and five times back to back. The calls had all been recent since we returned from Saint Thomas, up until the end of the statement which was a week ago. Calls at 1:00, 4:00 and 6:00 in the morning, crazy times all over the place. Sometimes they would talk for hours. I was livid. If it's over, then what the hell is he doing still talking to her and why the hell is he calling her at all hours of the night?

When Bernard finally came home, it was 9:00 that night. "Where have you been? Why didn't you call me back?" I asked. "What the fuck is wrong with you? No, I didn't get your message. My phone was dead. I need to charge it," he replied. He walked past me and went upstairs and started the shower. "Bernard, what the hell is this?" I showed him the phone bill. "What are you talking about? What are you doing Caryn, you tracking my calls now?" "Bernard, you must think that I'm an idiot, an idiot! Give me some credit, damn. I know Missy's number. I've seen it on our caller id and my damn caller id at work remember? I know her fucking number. What the hell are you calling her for Bernard? It's over, Caryn it's over blah blah blah. Isn't that what you said to me, assured me, Bernard?" My voice is raised and the tears are falling hard now.

"You know, Caryn, this is ridiculous. What you don't trust me, huh? I told you it was over and now you are snooping around trying to find something. I can't deal with this. I'm going out," and slams the bathroom door. When he comes out, he gets dressed, grabs his keys, and heads for the door. "Bernard, you're just going to leave? You're acting as if I did something wrong!" "Well, you are the fucking FBI now, right? I don't have time for this, I gotta go."

He stayed out all night. I called his cell phone I know five or six times. The first couple of times it just rang until his voice-mail came on. I called the last time around 3:00 am and it went directly into voice-mail. I slept for maybe one hour that night. At around 8:00 that next morning, I was all over the place. I didn't know what to do or what to think. I tried Bernard's phone again, but it still went directly into voice-mail. I called my Aunt Max and she said she would come right over. At around 10:00 my home phone rings. I just knew it was him, but it was Missy's number on the caller id. She didn't leave a message. Why is she calling here? Now I really don't know what to do. I needed to talk to Monica. I dialed her number.

"Hey girl! I was just thinking about you. I haven't really talked to you since you all grown and married now," Monica said jokingly. I didn't say anything, but just kind of muttered, "Yeah I know." "What's wrong Caryn, you don't sound like yourself?" "How are you and the twins doing in your tummy?" I asked trying to find the words to break my drama to her. "We're good. I'm just ready to push them out all ready! One of them is stomping on my kidneys now! What's going on girl?" Now in tears, I told her the whole story from how Bernard was acting this summer, the wedding, Missy, last night, everything. "And the bitch just called. Why is she calling here?" "Well did you call her back to see what she wanted?" Monica asked. "I can't call that girl. Bernard would kill..." "But he ain't there, right? Look, I can't tell you what to do, but if it were me I would see what she has to say. Stop crying and try to be objective. He's your husband. Sometimes the "ho" forgets that she's the "ho" and starts expecting shit from the man. Girl you've got to handle this, whatever this is."

I saw my Aunt Max pull up in the driveway. "My aunt is here. I'll call you back. Thanks for listening. Love you," I said, then hung up. I felt a little bit better after talking to her, calmer. Aunt Max walked in asking, "What in the world is going on up in here, Caryn?" "Miss Missy called here this morning, and I have not heard from Bernard all night." I'm more angrier now than sad. "Well did you talk to her?" "That's the same thing Monica said. No, I didn't talk to her. Her number came up on the call id. I didn't answer it. My Aunt Max didn't say anything. You think I should call her too?" "Why not? This is your house right? And she called your phone." "He's going to be pissed if he knew that I..." She cut me off and asked, "Now where did you say your husband was again?"

I dialed Bernard's number. This time it rang, but he still didn't answer. I dialed Missy's number next. "Hello," the voice said on the other end. "Is this Missy?" I asked. Hesitantly, she responded, "yes..... this is Missy." "Missy, this is Caryn, Bernard's wife.

I see that you have called my home, and I want to know why." Missy says, "Well, I called you because we really do need to talk. It has to come out. Bernard is still lying and cheating and I can't continue to live like this." "What do you mean still lying and cheating?" She continued, "Well, we are still seeing each other and have been since you all got back from the wedding. When he left here this morning, I told him that he needed to make a decision and stop this going back and forth."

I must admit that I was rather calm during my two hour long conversation with Missy. Something about the things she said led me to believe that she was not the one lying. Bernard was. She started at the beginning and gave me a detailed account of their four year relationship: "We met at a club in 1999. Bernard asked me to dance, asked for my number, and we started hanging out. My daughter took a liking to him and started to see him as a father figure. So, they would play together and we would do things together, like as a family. Sometimes we would go to DC and spend time with his dad and his family up there". I interrupted, "So he never mentioned me?" She continued, "Yes, he told me about you and that you lived in Richmond, but that he was going to end it with you after he and I met.

I really didn't know anything until he started acting funny towards the end of last year. He just stopped calling me all of a sudden, and I couldn't get in contact with him. I didn't know what had happened to him. I found out from one of his boys that you had moved back here and y'all had bought that house in Hampton. He heard from somebody, I don't know who, that I had gone out a couple of times with one of his friends, so he started calling me back in May around my birthday. I guess his jealousy couldn't keep him away. He said that you were the one that wanted to get married, and he was trying to figure out how to get out of it without hurting you. I believed him because I knew how much we loved each other. And then too, every time he would come over, he wanted to have sex like three and four times back to back. I just assumed y'all couldn't be hooking up because he was always asking me for it. I mean, I'm sure after all these years, you know how sexual he is. He is always talking about and wanting to have sex. And I mean anywhere too. Girl, when he first bought that truck, he kept talking about doing it in there. He got me though, and I must admit it was good. And then that sex tape that we did..." I cut her off. "I really don't need to hear that." That's what I said, but in my head I was thinking, "I really don't need to hear that, you ghetto bitch." "Well, I'm sorry. I just think you need to know about your husband," she said defensively. Something about the way she said "your husband" grated on my nerve. "Look I'd like to keep this as amicable as possible. I, we need to deal with him, not each other," I responded trying to remain calm and somewhat reasonable. I then thought to myself, I wonder if she even knows what the word amicable means?

Missy continued, "Well remember when Bernard would stay out last summer or get in late? He was with me most times. He would call you from my house and tell you that he was at Jay's, at a bar, or at some club. Remember when he got called back from being laid off from his job, and he told you he was working the night shift? He lied about that too. He told you that, but he was really living with me the whole time from probably August until after everything went down after the wedding.

The other thing is that I have a really big family, and they are close to Bernard too. He really was a big help to me and my mom doing that crazy ass hurricane back in September. He would take her to work and get water and groceries for the both of us. He really looked out for us then. And every holiday he has been right there with us for Christmas dinner, Thanksgiving dinner, it didn't matter. My family is wild as hell, but he was down with that cause his ass crazy too. I remember one time he had pissed me off because I couldn't reach him one weekend. I called and called, but he never called me back. When he finally called me, I wouldn't answer my phone. He called me for like two days non stop. After I wouldn't answer, he came by my house one night banging and kicking my door. I knew he would come which is why I didn't even bother about answering my phone or calling him back. I know him like a book. I went ahead and opened the door before somebody called the police. He was yelling asking me if I had some "mother fucker up in here and this was his shit" blah blah blah. I guess since he was paying my rent he felt like he owned the place. Bernard knows I don't take no crap and no disrespect from no man. He knows that I won't tolerate that shit he does to you. If my man stays out all night, he knows that when he gets home the damn locks will be changed.

So anyway, long story short, the night before you left for your wedding is when Bernard came to my house and told me that he was going through with the wedding, but that he loved me and my daughter and would always love us. He told me that after we made love, mind you. I was hurt and upset which is why I called you. My sister got all up in it too, and it just got worse. I mean he's been a part of our family for four years. And all of my peeps are pissed about what he did to me when he married you. I had cousins that wanted to come after him, but I ain't for no foolishness. I just thought it was time for me and you to talk. Bernard needs to make a choice because this is too crazy."

"Ah huh. Sounds like you've known about me since the beginning. Even after he chose to marry me, you still continued to mess with a married man. So why should I believe you?" I asked, still calm. "Cause I don't have nothing to loose at this point and because if you really look back over the last few years and be honest with yourself, you will see that I am telling you the truth," she replied adamantly and a bit cocky. "Ok, so maybe it's about time that we meet then and figure out what the hell to do next," I said surprisingly. "Cool, this should be fun," Missy responded. I'm thinking to myself this ain't no fucking game, what's fun about it?

We agreed to meet in an hour near where she lived. When I hung up the phone, my Aunt Max was at a loss for words. I took the wedding picture of the mantel and slammed it against the fireplace cracking its frame. "Are you sure you want to do this? Let me go with you to meet this woman," Aunt Max said. "No, I've got to handle this myself. I'll be ok. I'll call you later."

After Aunt Max left, I got dressed and hurried to meet the "other woman." Confusion. Mass confusion. I had been living in confusion and going through changes for months, and it wasn't over yet.

9

THERE'S A STRANGER IN MY HOUSE

I knew exactly where Missy lived. It was some Section 8 housing area about 15 minutes away. I guess Bernard would leave our lovely four bedroom single family home with the big back yard, the one that he found for us mind you and doted on when we first moved in, to go to his girlfriend's two bedroom apartment. Imagine that.

As I was pulling up in the grocery store parking lot, my cell phone rang. It was Bernard. I didn't answer it. Missy pulled up beside me. Her cell phone rang. She showed it to me so that I could see Bernard's number on the caller id. I told her to answer it. Missy put him on speaker. "What's up baby?" she answered. "Nothing, just checking on you," he said. "That thang sure was good last night. You coming back and give me some more of that tonight sexy?" she asked. Bernard responded, "Yeah it was good. We'll see." "Where's the wifey?" she asked him laughing. "Don't start with me Missy. I told you I was going to talk to her. Look I was just calling, I'm on my way home now." She hung up the phone and said, "He don't even have a clue." I could tell that she found this whole situation to be amusing. Although I was calm, I was actually sick to my stomach.

Missy wasn't what I had imagined. Petite, long hair, and light skinned, and maybe a few years younger than me. She was cute, but you could tell that she was a bit rough around the edges. To be honest, I am not sure what I had thought she'd look like. Tore up from the floor up would have been my preference. She must have known what I looked like or what I drove though because she damn sure pulled up right beside me and waved like we knew each other and like we were girls or something.

I brought some of our wedding pictures with me so that Missy could see that this man that she thought she knew was not the one that I knew. The man that married me was happy in St. Thomas, wanted me, wanted to spend the rest of his life with me, wanted to have babies with me. She looked at the pictures but didn't say anything. I could tell that even though she didn't say anything, she was taking it all in. The expression on her face said it all.

"So, what about the baby?" I asked. "Oh yeah, our baby. Bernard was so excited about having a boy. He went to all my doctor's appointments with me. He had even started to buy baby clothes with his silly self." "That's interesting, because he told me that he didn't even know if the baby was his," I said, staring her dead her in her face. She ignored my comment and continued, "I miscarried around the sixth month, Mother's Day weekend. He told me when ya'll got back from the wedding that he still wanted to have our baby." She said "our baby" with a rather spiteful tone almost as if she wanted to hurt me. I let it slide though. Mother's Day weekend. That was the weekend of my 10 year college reunion that Bernard said he couldn't take me to; the weekend that we had that big argument and broke up. I replied, "Interesting. You loose your baby and within a month he's up in Richmond telling me how much he loved me and asking me to marry him." I thought to myself so much for his so-called commitment to you Miss Missy.

My cell phone rang again for the third time. I still didn't answer, but this time Bernard left a voice-mail message. I put the phone on speaker so that Missy could hear. Bernard says, "Caryn, I'm sorry baby. I know you are upset about last night, but listen to me sweetheart. I stayed over Jay's last night because I needed to do some thinking about everything.

You know how much I love you. You are my wife, baby. Ain't nobody else but you. Straight from the heart, straight from the heart. Let's talk when you get home. Dinner will be waiting for you when you get here."

I could tell that Missy was pissed while she listened to his voice-mail message. "Now does that sound like a man that is coming home to tell me that he wants to be with you and that is over with us?" I asked her rhetorically. Missy responded, "That mother fucker. He's been playing both of us. He's good, I've got to give it to him." "And I think its time that we play his ass. He's at home, so let's go," I said. "Ok, I'm right behind you," she replied.

I called Monica while I was driving home and told her that I had met Missy and that we were on our way to confront Bernard. As I was talking to her, my voice cracked as I tried to hold back the tears. Monica said, "Oh girl, don't cry! It's going to be ok. I know it's hard, but you do what you need to do! Just be careful cause you don't know how he's going to react. Expect the unexpected." I then called my Aunt Max to let her know what was up, just in case I needed her. I really didn't know what to expect nor did I have a plan. All I knew was that Bernard was finally going to get a taste of his own game, and that I'm not the naive, fool that he thought I was.

My cell phone rang again. This time Bernard's message sounded like he was upset with me. "Caryn, where are you? I've been calling you but you're not answering your phone. Call me at home," and he slams down the phone. As we approach my subdivision, Missy calls. "Do you want me to park on another street?" "No, just pull up behind me in the driveway."

What happens next was so surreal, it really is a blur. When Missy and I pulled up and before we could get out of our cars, Bernard ran out of the house and went straight for Missy. He grabbed her, and was trying to force her back in her car. She got away from him and tried to continue up towards the house with me, but he shoved her. He then looked at me with a glare I'd never seen before and told me to get in the house. His tone was so fierce that it scared me a little. Missy didn't give up trying to get in the house. He snatched her arm and pulled it behind her. I heard her yelling "Ouch. Bernard you're hurting me." He let her go, but then started cussing and yelling at her. "What the fuck you doing, huh? Coming to my house? Teaming up with my wife? Have you lost your damn mind, Missy?" "Bernard, this is some bull shit. You've been lying to her, lying to me, and it ain't right. You telling me all this shit about how you love me and my daughter and that you don't want her. Don't you put your hands on me again, I've told your ass that before!" Now at this point, I'm thinking to myself so, he's put his hands on her before? "Missy you need to get the fuck out of here now. Don't be bringing this shit to my house!" He's now yelling at the top of his lungs. Now she's yelling, "Caryn, you are crazy if you stay with his ass! You think he's just fucking me? Hell no! I'm not the only one, trust me. Damn you, Bernard!" she screams before she pulls out of the driveway.

While all of this was going on I was hoping that the neighbors wouldn't call the police. It felt like I was a part of some ghetto talk show episode. I mean, please. I went upstairs and packed a small bag while they were still out there going at it. I heard Bernard come up the stairs. I held my breath. I was expecting him to come at me like he did with Missy. Calmly he said, "Caryn, baby, why did you bring her here? You don't bring no woman up in your house. You can't trust her." Now, I'm not sure who this person was that came upstairs, because he was rather composed and apologetic, not defensive, aggressive, ranting and raving like the one who was just outside with Missy. Dr. Jekyll and Mr. Hyde?

I looked at him as if he was some stranger. "You say I can't trust her. I know everything; she gladly and I must say proudly told me everything. I know about how you met, how you and she did the family thing with her freaking kid. I know about when she lost *your* baby. I know how you've been seeing her damn near this whole year and how you have this crazy passionate sex three and four times back to back anywhere and everywhere including in the truck I bought!

I know that you always crying broke, but seem to find money or should I say use my money to wine and dine Missy. She told me about the hotel rooms, the trips, the gifts, and I hear you paying folks rent now huh?

Let's see, what else do I fucking know? I can't forget this, I know that you lied and told me that you were working the night shift while you were really living with Missy. I know that one month, one month before our wedding you were taking care of her damn family during and after the hurricane while I came home alone every night for a fucking week with no electricity, no water, no nothing. I know that you told her how you loved her and her kid the night before we left for St. Thomas. I know that you fucked her last night even though you told me you were at Jay's. Don't even try to deny it. She had your ass on speakerphone, so I heard you say it. I know that you started back seeing her one week after our wedding even though you told me it was over. The tears are streaming down my face now like a never ending waterfall, but I continue. What I know is that you are a pathological liar, and have been lying to me since the day we met, since day one."

For once, Bernard had a look of defeat on his face. Defeat, but not surrender. "Ok Caryn you got me. I have a problem, but I can fix it. I'll do whatever you want me too. I'll go to counseling this time, for real. I'll leave her alone I swear, I'll leave her alone. I need you, I love you Caryn. Don't leave me. He then falls down on his knees with tears falling, please don't leave me sweetheart, please. I ain't never begged anybody for anything ever, but I am on my knees begging you."

I looked at him with contempt. "Bernard, how could you do this to me? I have loved you with everything I have and everything I know since I was twenty years old, for thirteen years Bernard, thirteen years. I don't know you, I thought I knew you. She, she, Missy knows you..." I picked up my bag and headed for the stairs. He grabbed my arm and responded, "Caryn, you do know me. It's me, look in my eyes. It's me. You said it, thirteen years we have together. It's all my fault, I admit it. Just give me one more chance, that's all I ask. I'll do anything." He sounded so sincere and he looked like he'd lost his best friend. "I need to go, to get away. I just can't be here right now, it's just too much," I replied. "Caryn just leave the bag here, just come back please," he said looking pitiful. I knew he was going to give me a hard time if I took the bag, so I just said anything so I could get out of there. I needed to breathe.

I got in the car and sped out of there just as fast as I could. My head, my mind was spinning. Who is this man? Did I really know Bernard Williams? He's been living separate lives as long as I don't know when. What kind of man, what kind of person would do this? He was a stranger. I had been living with and sleeping with a stranger. What do I do now?

10

S I L L Y

Fool. Defined as a stupid or silly person; a person who lacks judgment or sense. Was I a fool all of these years? How could I have misjudged Bernard's character, his moral fiber? Was I blind or just plain stupid? That's the million dollar question. How silly of me was it to think that Bernard could be committed to me, only me? How silly of me was it to not see, not acknowledge the warning signs?

As I reflect back over the years, it all seems clearer now and makes sense. Like the first day we met. Bernard lied and told me that he was living with Jay when he was really living with his girlfriend all along. When he finally came clean, he told me that they were not together and that he was just trying to get himself together to move out. Little did I know that this lie would be the first lie in a serious of lies that would eventually come crashing down on me.

Like the first time he didn't show up for a date and didn't call until two days later. He said that he had a bad cold and was too sick to call. Like when we went all through Christmas break that first year that we met without talking. He didn't call me not one time while I was in Richmond until after I returned back to college in January. He said that he'd lost my number and of course couldn't call from his home phone (he was living with his so called ex girlfriend) but knew that we would hook back up when I got back to Hampton.

Or when he didn't attend my graduation, my most proud moment, because he said it was Mother's Day and he was spending it with his aunt and grandmother that lived out of town and how difficult Mother's Day was for him since his mom had died; like the many times when we would go for a week or two without talking when I lived in Richmond. I'd call and leave messages, but could never reach him. When he'd finally call me, he'd say that he was working overtime or nights and was just tired. How about the many times that he had promised to come visit me in Richmond and he never showed or called.

Or how about the time when I drove down to Hampton from Richmond to visit him one evening after work. He knew that he would still be at work when I got there, so he told me to let myself in with the spare key that I had. I had only been there about an hour, and his phone rang. I just knew it was him checking to see if I had gotten there safely. To my surprise, it wasn't him, but a woman with a New York accent. She asked to speak to him, and I told her that he wasn't there and asked if I could take a message for him. She said, "Is this his girlfriend Caryn?" I slowly said "Y-e-s." She then said her name and proceeded to tell me that she was his other girlfriend too. I was like "Excuse me?" She went on to tell me that he would visit her sometimes in New York and she would visit sometimes in Hampton.

When Bernard got home from work, I told him what had happened. He basically chastised me for answering his phone and invading his privacy. He then denied everything she said. He said that she was just a friend that he'd met and that she wanted more than just friendship. He said he hadn't talk to her in months and that she was fucking with me to get me upset. He said "If she was supposed to be my girlfriend, then why would I tell her about you? How would she know your name? If I was going to cheat, believe me she wouldn't know anything about you." I don't know how he did it but by the time the conversation was over, I felt like I had done something wrong by accusing him. I still made love to him that night even though there was this nagging feeling in the back of my mind that something was not right.

Oh and I have to mention all of the missed birthdays and holidays that we never spent together. I can count on my finger, on one hand, the number of birthday and Christmas gifts that I received over the thirteen years that we dated. Or like the Valentine's Days that passed year after year that I spent alone with no word or no gift from him. "I had to work, I don't feel good, I'm going over Jay's, I worked last night and I don't feel like driving all the way to Richmond, I don't have any money" were the excuses he gave for years for not spending those special times with me.

And oh, once he declared his undying love for me and asked me to marry him, the signs were there too. Like the nights that he didn't come home, or came home in the wee hours of the morning. Like the times when he would leave "going to the store" and would be gone for hours. I would call and call, but he would never answer his phone. It would ring or go directly into voice-mail. Like when his cell phone would ring and he wouldn't answer it in my presence, or when he would take the cell phone into the bathroom with him and talk in a deep, low whisper.

And like so many instances when he would be moody and wouldn't want to talk and would get defensive when I asked where he'd been. Like when he wasn't working and he stayed gone all of the time, would ask me for money and would spend it all on going out "with the fellas." Like two weeks before our wedding he asked me if I would leave him if he told me that he wanted to wait longer and get married later...

I stayed over my Aunt Max's house that evening. I just needed to go somewhere away from that house, my house and just think. Bernard called over and over again, but I just couldn't talk to him yet. His dad called me too. Evidently, Bernard had confided in him and the two cooked up this scheme to try to convince me to come home and give Bernard another chance. Although I didn't to talk to Bernard, I did talk to his dad. I was curious to see just how much Mr. Williams knew about his son and Miss Missy. After listening to the how "men just sometimes get caught up in the streets" talk from Mr. Williams, I just cut him off point blank. "You knew about her all along. You invited and entertained Missy into your home, your momma's home, your brother's, everybody in the whole Williams family had her over at all the freaking family functions for years! You knew that he wasn't ready to marry me, but you went along with this charade and look what happened? Not only was he not ready to marry me, he was got dammit in love with someone else! How could you let him do this? You've been telling me for years and years how I was the best person for him, how much you thought of me as a daughter, how we were family. He didn't have to marry me, he could have married her!!! I guess you all think of me as the biggest fool! The joke's been on me and all of you knew, everybody knew." Now the tears are falling and my voice is rising.

He responded, "I know you are upset baby, and I don't blame you. It was not my place to tell you about Bernard. He's my son. I asked him if you were the one Caryn, and he told me yes. I told him then that he needed to end it with her. I know he messed up, but I believed him then when he told me that he loved and wanted you to be his wife, and I still believe him. I can't tell you what to do, it's your decision. Bernard deserves whatever happens to him. I would ask that you go home when you are ready, and just hear him out. Then make your decision. Believe me when I tell you that you are the best thing that has ever happened to him, and he's the fool, not you, if he messes what you all have up."

My head was hurting and eyes were hurting from crying so much. I remember my mom telling me years ago that there is always one person in a relationship that loves the other more. I didn't want to believe that love wasn't 50/50 in a relationship. The truth is that I did love Bernard more than he loved me. It was apparent in the way he treated me; his actions, not his words. Funny how things become crystal clear to you way too late. How silly of me to think all these years that Bernard loved me as much as I loved him. Just damn silly.

11

STOP IN THE NAME OF LOVE

Being at Aunt Max's house last night was good for me. She made us the best strawberry banana daiquiris topped with whip cream and tiny pieces of fresh strawberries. We just chilled by the fireplace for most of the evening. We talked a little, chilled a little, cried a little. I had to turn my phone off because Bernard kept calling me and leaving messages begging me to come home.

I went back home the next morning. I wasn't sure what to expect and really didn't know what I wanted to say. I have always been a planner, but this was one conversation that even I couldn't map out. As I pulled in the driveway, I started to feel angry.

You know like boiling water kind of angry. You know when you see that water is boiling so hard that you can feel its intensity, its heat? So much that you rush to the stove to turn the heat down? That's how I felt as I looked at our neighborhood, our yard, our beautiful home. The home that Bernard chose to leave and go lay up in the projects and... Ok, stop it. I'm not going to go there, I'm not going to go there.

Bernard opened the front door before I could even get out of the car good. When I walked in, he grabbed me and tried to hug me, but I pushed him away. "Thank God, Caryn. You had me worried. I've been calling you and calling you all night. Thank God you came back home. Please talk to me sweetheart."

I still was at a loss for words. For the first time, this didn't feel like home. I kept looking around the house like I was looking for something, but just didn't know what. "Say something please," he said. "You told me for weeks that you were working the night shift. I spent all of those nights alone thinking that my man was at work. The hurricane, I mean the hurricane. How could you leave me at home to fend for myself with no lights, no electricity? In the dark by myself? Some of those days I never saw you at all because you would be "gone" to work by the time I got home from work in the evening, and when I would leave for Richmond at the crack of dawn in the morning, you claimed that you would get home after I had already left. Now that I think about it, I remember asking you point blank if you had been home one of those days. I knew something was off, and something told me that you had not been home. But, you told me one of your lies as usual. The whole time you were not only staying with Missy but taking care of her and her family, Bernard? I mean we didn't even have water for the first couple of days. My God anything could have happened to me here by myself, and you didn't even care!"

"That's not true, that's not true. Yes, I was staying with her. I was wrong for that I know, and if I could change what I did I would. He dropped his head. But I can't take it back, Caryn I can't. There was a pause. Ok. I knew you were going to be safe here and that nothing was going to happen to you. She, her, her mom, they (clearing his throat) needed help. I mean she has a kid and I just felt like..." "You felt like what? I was your fiancé remember? Not her. You chose to leave your home to help the whore? What does that say about us, your respect or lack thereof for me?" He didn't answer.

"It's all been one big lie from day one Bernard, our whole relationship. The beginning, the middle, and now all a lie. You are a lie. What gets me is that you didn't have to marry me. I asked you, I asked you Bernard before we left for St. Thomas if you were sure. You said you were. Why did you marry me, you didn't have to marry me?" "Because I wanted to make you happy Caryn," he said. "Make me happy? I thought you married me because you loved me!"

"I did, I do. I'm just saying that I knew what I had done and I wanted to make things right. I just thought getting married would make things right."

"For some reason you can't leave her alone. You've been with her for four years. You just told me what a minute ago that it was over with Missy. I mean you went back to her right after we got married and was with her night before last. What the hell is wrong with you? Why don't you just be with her if that's what you want? I mean what have I been doing wrong? Was her pussy better than mine, what? He looked at me with this shameful look and said, "Caryn, stop." "I mean she makes it seem like ya'll be doing it anytime anywhere. I'm serious Bernard, what's wrong with me? Am I not pretty enough, freaky enough? What makes you want to be with her over and over and over again even after you married me?"

"It's not you Caryn. You've been everything to me and for me. You were there even when my family wasn't; when I lost my job, my confidence, when I had no money. It may not seem like it to you right now, but I do love you and everything about you. You are about as pure and perfect as anyone can be. Missy could never be the person you are. I just got caught up in something that I thought I could handle. This thing has just gotten out of control." One single tear falls down his cheek.

"But you still have not told me what it is that she's been doing that I haven't. What is it about her?" There was a long pause. With his head down, he replied, "I don't know what to say Caryn." "Ok, well there has to be a reason. People just don't mess around unless something is wrong or they're not happy at home." He still wouldn't say anything. "Ok Bernard it's obvious that you want to be with her and that she's giving you whatever it is that I'm not. I mean she almost had your baby for God sake. You two share something deeper than what you want to admit to yourself or even to me. Bernard, we've been friends for a long time and maybe you feel some sense of obligation to me or something. If Missy's the one you truly want, then you need to be with her. You do. I love you enough to let you go. I will be ok, don't worry about me."

"But I don't want to loose you, Caryn. I want you, not her." "You keep freaking telling me that! But you keep going back to her, and you won't even tell me why. You know Bernard, all I've been thinking about were these red flags that were waving around knocking me in the head all along. Missy told me about how you all went to Florida for her birthday last year, and all of the holidays you've spent together. She even talked about her annual family reunion that you have always been a part of. Ok, in thirteen years, I can count on one hand the number of holidays you spent with me. And you ain't been to not one of my family reunions, notta one. Remember the 50th birthday party I gave my mom and you called me at the last minute and told me that you didn't feel like coming? I mean as mad as I was at you, I still forgave you. You didn't even have enough respect for me or value our relationship enough to be there to celebrate my mother's birthday. I mean all the times you reneged on dates, on weekends. All the times I couldn't reach you for days, weeks sometimes. All the times you came home late or didn't come home at all. What more evidence did I need? I mean damn. You, all y'all must think that I am the biggest idiot!"

Bernard looked me dead in my eyes and replied, "Caryn, I fucked up. I admit and can't deny it. But while you're taking this walk down memory lane, think about the good times, the times I remember. I remember the first day we met and how all I wanted was to get to know this pretty brown thang with that perfect shaped ass named Caryn Harris; I remember the Christmas that I surprised you and showed up at your cousin's house in Richmond for dinner; I remember when I took you to your college senior ball; the weekends we spent at the beach, the times we spent at my dad's in Maryland, how much fun we had when we went to see the Pittsburgh game live, the Washington game too, that ski trip in West Virginia making love in that jacuzzi, the time I helped your girl Tammy move, the day we moved into this house and how we talked about our future and our babies, the times we made love, Saint Thomas, our marriage vows til death do us part. Yeah, it's been thirteen years, I know that. But I just want you to remember the good times too, Caryn. Because there were some good times."

Damn he's good, I have to give it to him. My mind went back to that ski trip and the jacuzzi, the heat, the force of the jets, his body pressed up against mine... I responded, "The good times is what has kept me here even when the nagging feeling in the depth of my soul told me otherwise. This is just too much Bernard. We haven't even been married two months yet, and here we are." "Caryn, please just don't leave me. Give me another chance. I told you that I will do whatever you want me to do, I swear to God. You still love me?" Why does he do that? "Bernard, please. I don't know what to do. I really don't. This is some bullshit. Maybe we need to talk to somebody, get counseling or something." "Ok baby, we can do that. Make us another appointment, and I'm there."

By this time, I am mentally and physically exhausted. I barely slept last night at my Aunt Max's and then had to deal with him first thing this morning. We talked what seem liked forever and the hours just went by. Bernard said he would order a pizza. Something about eating pizza for Sunday dinner just ain't right, just ain't Christian. But hell, I was in no mood to cook nothing for nobody. I would have been perfectly happy with a bowl of cream of wheat.

Bernard looked at TV downstairs and played video games for most of the evening. He came upstairs to the bedroom I guess around 9:00 and started taking his clothes off. I told him that I thought we needed to separate for awhile and that I was going back to Richmond. He didn't say anything, but moved towards the bed. "Bernard, don't. Please sleep downstairs." He looked at me as if he was about to say something; but he stopped himself, grabbed a blanket from the linen closet, and went on downstairs.

12

YOU'RE GONNA MAKE ME LOVE SOMEBODY ELSE

This was the longest weekend ever. For it to have only been two days, it felt like two weeks. Bernard got up early Monday morning and left for work. I pretended to be moving around as if I was getting ready to go to work too, but I had already decided that I was going to call in sick and stay home. If Bernard knew that I was staying home, he would ask me a thousand questions, and he might have tried to stay home with me. I couldn't face anybody today. I barely slept the last three nights, and I just needed to be alone. The truth was that I was sick; sick to my damn stomach. Bernard tried to kiss me goodbye, but I turned away from him. He mumbled, "I'll see you later. I'm sorry Caryn that I hurt you."

After he left, I took a long, hot bubble bath and soaked by candlelight. The peppermint scented candles tended to sooth and relax me, so I thought that would be good for me right about now. My mind kept going back to everything that had gone down since the wedding and especially what went down with Missy this weekend; meeting her, talking to her, hearing about the man that I thought I knew. We got married in October and it's not even Thanksgiving yet. What do I do, what do I do? I prayed, I meditated, I prayed some more. By the time I got out of the tub, I may have looked like a prune but I felt like I at least knew what my next step should be.

I ate some oatmeal and drank some orange juice for breakfast. I decided to pull out the big guns; I called my father. I told him the whole story starting from when I first got the voice-mail messages from Missy and her sister. "I can't believe you have been going through this for weeks by yourself. I couldn't even tell anything was wrong. Baby girl, I'm so sorry. Wow, this is tough, but you're strong and you will get through it. Have you decided what you're going to do?" "I think I need to go back home for awhile. Bernard said he would go to counseling. I don't know if it will help, but I am going to set up an appointment for us when I get off the phone with you. He assures me that it's over with Missy and that he wants to make this right with us. Daddy, what do you think?" "Counseling is a start, but it only works if both parties are truly open to being helped. I'm not going to lie to you baby girl, but Bernard has some serious issues that won't be resolved overnight, if ever. I support whatever decision you make. But I think you are doing the right thing."

I felt like a weight had been lifted after talking to my dad. His words of wisdom and support were what I needed. I tried to handle this mess myself, but after what happened this weekend, I really needed to get some advice from a man, and my daddy was the only man that I could trust with this drama. He didn't sugar coat it, he talked to me both from a man's point of view and a father's.

After I finished talking to him, I watched the soaps. The soap operas was like the best diversion for me because I was able to temporarily forget what was going on in my life and vicariously live through the actor's lives. I fell asleep after the soaps went off and slept for a good two and a half hours. When I woke up, I called my employee assistance program and set up an appointment with a marriage counselor for Bernard and me. As soon as I hung up the phone, I heard the house alarm go off. Bernard was back home from work.

I held my breath as I walked downstairs. Bernard was in the living room taking his coat off. He looked up at me as I came down the steps. Before he could say anything I said, "Bernard, I think we need to separate for awhile. I'm going back to Richmond until I can clear my head. I made an appointment for

us on Friday at 5:00 in Richmond with a counselor."
"So you're just going to leave like that? I mean how
long are you going to be gone? I can see a couple of
weeks maybe even a month, but you make it sound
indefinite. Caryn, baby I told you I will go with you
to counseling. I'll even keep sleeping downstairs, but
don't go. That ain't going to help this." "I have to
Bernard. Way too much has happened. For my sanity,
I need to get away, get away from here." I started
to go back upstairs when he grabbed my arm and
pulled me close to him. "Ok Caryn, you do what you
need to do. But this is temporary, ok? Temporary." I
let him continue to hug me. It was like a tug of war
inside me. Part of me wanted to pull away, part of
me still wanted to feel close to him. The part that
wanted to feel close to him won. Crazy I know.

I went to work the next morning. I slept the whole
van ride to Richmond. Being at work was actually
good for me. I was able to forget about the home
drama. It was like my Calgon. My dad called me
first thing to check on me. Bernard called me too.
I didn't answer, but he left a voice-mail telling me
how sorry he was for everything and how sure he was
that we were going to work through this separation.
"I love you Caryn," was the last thing he said. I felt a
twinge between my legs. Even after everything that
I learned this weekend, his telling me that he loved
me still gave me that woozy like feeling.

I had lunch with some of my co-workers downtown
which was fun. We went to the Trout Spot which is

one of the best restaurants in Richmond. I ordered my favorite: two piece fried fish, potatoes, cabbage, and corn bread. Luckily nobody asked me about married life, and I didn't volunteer no information. I was still a newlywed so folks probably assumed that I was still in honeymoon land. Not!

Bernard was there when I got home that evening. He was in his usual spot in the living room playing video games. I changed clothes and then went right in the kitchen to make dinner. I had a taste for spaghetti, so I decided on that and broccoli. Midway through cooking, Bernard came into the kitchen. "When are you leaving?" "Probably after Thanksgiving," I responded. Thanksgiving was in a couple of weeks. I wanted to wait a few more weeks because I wasn't ready to tell anybody about the separation. The thought of the embarrassment and the shame was too much. I mean we had only been married a little over a month. What would people think? What would they say?

Bernard slept in the downstairs bedroom the rest of the week. Friday morning, I reminded him that our appointment was at 5:00. I told him that I was going to drive my car to work instead of riding the van and for him to meet me at my job by 4:15. "Bernard, did you remember to take this afternoon off because you're going to need to leave work no later than 2:30 to beat the traffic and everything to get to Richmond?" "Yeah," he said rather hesitantly. "I'll see you later," he said and walked out the door.

I was really busy at work today. Around noon, my cell phone rang. It was Bernard's stepmother. "Hey Mrs. Williams." "Hi Caryn. I just wanted to tell you that I left Bernard's dad, and I am filing for divorce." "What? What happened?" "I don't want to get into it, but I thought that I owed it to you to call. This is not the first time I've left him, but it is damn sure the last time. You know I never had any children of my own, but I have always respected you and loved you like a daughter. The apple doesn't fall far from the tree. Lies, deceit, abuse, alcohol. I'll leave it at that. You have to make the best decision for you. I know it's hard especially when your heart is all up in the mix of it. Been there, done that, and done with it. I just wanted to call you and tell you that you are in my prayers." That was it. She hung up. She's leaving Bernard's dad? I can't believe it. They always seemed so happy. I mean I knew that he drank too, but what did she mean about lies, deceit, and abuse and the apple falling from the tree? Within a few months, their divorce was final. Too much, just too much.

My mom was off today, so I went by her house for lunch and broke the news to her. "Dogs, men are all dogs! Just no good. Well, I think you are doing the right thing by leaving him. If a man cheats on you once, he'll do it again. And listen to his stepmother. Sounds like she knows the real deal! I'm sorry you are hurting, but you will be ok. God is always in control," she said while hugging me tight. One thing is for sure. Looks like my mother will be the first one to show up to help me move! After lunch, we chatted awhile longer, then I headed back to work.

I had a meeting right at 2:00 which lasted about an hour. When I got back to my desk, I saw where Bernard had called me a couple of times, but didn't leave a message. He called me again around 3:30 from our house phone. "How's your day?" he asked. "It's been ok. Are you about to get on the road? We are going to be late to our counseling session." There was that damn pause. "Uhmm, Caryn. I'm not ready to talk to a stranger about my personal business. I thought I could do it, but I can't, not yet. Give me a couple of weeks." "Bernard, you promised! You think this is some easy shit that we can fix? Just come on please, just one appointment. Let's just see what he says," I said tears now falling. "See, you're crying now. What's going to happen when we get into that office? What does he know? He don't know me, and I don't need nobody fucking judging me. I can't Caryn. Sorry." He hung up. I tried to call him back but he didn't answer.

Now what? Do I go ahead and go by myself? I called my dad in tears: "Daddy, he won't go. He told me he would go." "Go where baby?" he asked. "To counseling. Our appointment is this evening, remember?" I was trying to get myself together because I was still at work. "Well maybe you should go ahead and go so you can talk this thing out with someone objective," he said. "I thought you were objective," I said now smiling. "I'm trying to be baby girl, but this is rough on me too. You're hurting, so I'm hurting. I wouldn't want to see Bernard on the street right about now." I couldn't tell if he was serious or not, but I think he meant it.

At 5:00 p.m., I'm sitting in the waiting room for this counselor Mr. Washington. He came and got me about five minutes later. Ok, he must have been related to Denzel Washington, because his ass was fine! I almost forgot all my problems and the reason why I was there in the first place. Tall, nice build, salt and pepper hair and beard, smooth skin. He looked like he could be in his early 50's. He looked good for an older dude. When he opened his mouth, he sounded like those sensual DJ's on the quiet storm radio. Now I see why women be falling all in love with their therapists!

The first thing he asked me was where my husband was. I told him the truth that Bernard was a private person and didn't want to talk to a stranger. After he asked me a serious of general questions, he then told me to tell him what was going on. I started with Saint Thomas and ended up with Bernard reneging on coming to this meeting today. By the time I had finished the story, I had used up almost the whole box of Kleenex tissues that was on the table. "...and excuse my French but what the hell am I doing here? Crazy people see therapists. I'm not crazy. I'm not supposed to be here! This is what this man has brought me down to, going to see a freaking therapist. What the hell?" The tears are now falling faster than I can catch them with my tissues. Mr. Washington pulled out another box and handed it to me.

Before I knew it, my hour was up. Mr. Washington told me that he wanted me to come back next week so that I can go back further and tell him about the history of my relationship with Bernard prior to us getting married. I really didn't feel like I got any real counseling like talking about it, but I think the first session was more for the counselor to hear what the situation was. He took notes, and asked me a few follow up questions. I guess I was expecting him to fix the problem or something in one visit, so I wouldn't have to come back. Well, I guess it was official. I am now "in counseling." The thought of it just pissed me off even more. Here I am wasting my time. Well at least he was good to look at, good eye candy. That helped.

As I drove home, I reflected on my session with Mr. Washington and some of the questions he asked me. Having to tell my story made me feel embarrassed, ashamed, and like a complete idiot. How could I have let this happen? Why didn't I just kick Bernard's ass to the curb a long time ago?

I got home around 7:30 that evening. He wasn't there. I fixed myself a sandwich with chips and watched the Young & the Restless on the VCR. I called Monica to see how she was doing with her pregnancy and everything. Her doctor put her on bed rest for the rest of the pregnancy. She was due late January. We talked for awhile more about what was going on with her. I couldn't bring myself to talk about Bernard so I just told her that I would talk to her later.

I woke up when I heard the house alarm go off around 11:30 that night. I heard Bernard moving around downstairs in the kitchen. He came upstairs a few minutes later, took his clothes off, and got in the bed. Now he had been sleeping downstairs in the guest bedroom for over the last week, so not sure why he figured things had changed tonight. I was still mad at him for punking out and not going to see the counselor Mr. Washington today too.

"What are you doing?" I asked him. He had been drinking. He smelled like someone had dumped a whole bottle of gin on him. "This is my mother fucking bed too. You wanted to be married, so we married, so I gets to sleep in my bed with my wife," he responded all in one big slur. I went to get up, and he pulled me back down in the bed beside him. "Come on Mrs. Williams. This what married folks do. I ain't sleeping downstairs no more!" "Bernard, let me go! I'll go downstairs then. Just let me go!" I yelled. "Caryn, don't do this. I told you that I was sorry about everything. I know, I know you mad at me about not going to Richmond today, but I can handle all this. I can fix all this baby. Just trust me one last time. I mean you say you leaving and then all this shit with Missy. Just let me sleep in my bed here with you please Caryn. You feel so good."

God he smelled. I just gave up and let him hold me. He soon fell asleep. I laid there thinking. Should I leave? If I do leave, how long should I stay away? Should I stay with my mom? Should I stay with Tammy? No, if I stay with Tammy then I'd have to tell her. What if I just stay here and try to work things out with him? That way nobody would ever know. He seems so sincere. I know he's hurting too. Should I forgive him? Doesn't the bible say that we should forgive?

The next morning, Bernard got up to go to work. It was hard to believe that a whole week had gone by since last Saturday's episode. I stayed in bed sleeping off and on for most of the morning. I woke up when the phone rang. It was Bernard. "Good morning. I, I was just checking on you. You think we can go out to dinner or something this evening when I get off?" "I really don't feel up to it Bernard. We need to talk." "Well, I'll go by that seafood place you like and get take-out for dinner. I'll see you later. I love you Caryn." I didn't say anything. He then asked, "You love me? You still love me?" God, he's been doing that for years. It doesn't ever matter how mad I am at him. I don't know what it is, but the way he says "you love me" just makes me want to melt. What the hell is wrong with me? Whipped just whipped. I was able to mumble an "uh huh." He said goodbye and hung up.

Today must have been check on Caryn day because my mom, dad, Monica, Aunt Max, and Bernard's dad all called me. I didn't have a lot to say to Bernard's dad. He didn't mention that his wife had left him, so neither did I. I just listened as he still tried to plead his son's case. I told my Aunt Max I would pick her up tomorrow morning so we could go to church together. I still didn't have the energy to go into detail with Monica about Bernard, but told her that we would definitely catch up soon and how I appreciated her concern for me.

I decided to do a little cleaning at least upstairs anyway. I did our bathroom and dusted and vacuumed the bedroom. There's something about a fresh smelling house. Lemon pine. It seemed to perk me up some.

By the time Bernard came home, it was about 5:00. He had picked up fried fish and oyster dinners with macaroni & cheese and greens for the sides. I was starving, so that take-out was right on time. He made small talk about his day at work and some little story about the bar that he went to last night. That bar thing was the perfect lead in for me. "So what was wrong with you last night?" "What do you mean?" he asked looking or trying to look dumbfounded. "Bernard, come on now. First of all, you have been saying all week how you will do anything to fix this mess of yours including going to counseling. You left me hanging yesterday. And then you wouldn't even answer the phone when I called you back. Then you show up here last night pissy drunk forcing yourself on me." "Hold up Caryn. You act like I tried to rape you or something. What do you mean forced?" "You demanded to sleep upstairs after I had asked you to stay downstairs and then you held me down, yes against my will, in the bed so that I could not get up." "Ok, maybe it was the alcohol. I don't know. I do know that I didn't hurt you. I just wanted to hold you. It's been so long..." "It ain't been long for you. Did you forget that you fucked Missy last Friday? Nope, it ain't been long at all," I said sarcastically. "You Caryn, I'm talking about you, my wife." "Whatever. What about yesterday's appointment?" I asked again since he seemed to want to skirt over it.

"I already told you. I ain't letting nobody judge me. I caused the mess and I'm going to uncause it. I mean what do you want from me? I'm home, I'm here, I'm trying. Damn." "Why are you getting mad at me Bernard? This is all because of you, not me!" I'm crying now. There was a dead silence. His cell phone rang and broke the silence. He looked at it, but didn't answer. After he ate, he went into the living room and started playing video games on the play station. Not sure what I expected but the talk, as you can see, did not go very well.

The next couple of weeks or so went by pretty uneventful. Bernard never did go back to sleeping downstairs. I had promised him that I would not move back home until after Thanksgiving which was about another week or so away. I did have my second appointment with Mr. Washington which was just as draining as the first one. I still used up all of that man's tissues. I took him back to when Bernard and I first met and gave him a pretty good detailed snapshot of our whole relationship starting with day one. Mr. Washington was cool. I don't typically open up to people like talking about it, but there was something about him that made me feel comfortable and relaxed. I made another appointment for after Thanksgiving.

One night, Bernard came to bed and started telling me how much he loved me and how he was going to make things up to me. "I'm sorry Caryn. I never wanted to hurt you like this. You know you are the one for me." "Well it's painfully obvious that I'm not the one for you Bernard." "Let me show you. Let me show you that you are enough for me and that you are the one I want. It's been a long time since I made love to you the way you like it. You smell so good." He then started rubbing my shoulders, lightly kissing my breasts, and then I felt his fingers massaging me in that oh so sensitive area. My body started to respond to him before my brain could stop me. I just needed to feel, feel that closeness. I needed a release. Things have been so tense, and I've been so stressed. God, that feels so good. What is he doing to me? One thing's for sure, he was a master in the bedroom. All of your problems just seem to melt away, even if just for a sweet moment.

Neither one of us felt like going anywhere or facing anybody Thanksgiving. We both cooked and had a nice quiet holiday at home. I must admit it was nice being in the kitchen with him joking around. Maybe we can put all this stuff behind us, right? Maybe if I just stay in counseling that will help me to cope, right? This was the first time really since we got married that I actually felt married.

Bernard's cell phone kept ringing until he finally cut it off. The house phone rang a couple of times but they both were hang-ups. "Who was that?" I asked. "Wrong number, he replied." Something about those calls bothered me and I couldn't shake this uneasy feeling.

Bernard fell asleep watching the game. I went upstairs and turned on his cell phone. His contact list looked strange. He had one letter initials instead of the full name with the contact number. One was listed as "S", another was listed as "K". Was this some kind of code or something? Why not spell out the whole name? I checked the dialed calls and S and K were dialed on a regular almost around the same time. When I looked at received calls, S came up a few times.

Bernard left for work early Friday morning, black Friday. I had the day off. My mother came to visit and she, my Aunt Max, and I did some black Friday shopping. I needed the diversion because I still had that uneasy feeling about those strange code names in Bernard's phone. We had a nice day shopping. We all ended up buying suits from Lacy's. I bought a pair of jeans too.

After my mom went back to Richmond, I decided to catch up on some reading. Bernard called around 6:00. He told me that he was going out with a co-worker over in Norfolk and was going to stay over the co-worker's house since they would be out late. "Huh? Who is this guy? You've never mentioned him before." "Look Caryn, I just need some time to myself to think. This thing with us is still getting to me and it's still not right with us. I heard you crying in the bathroom last night. I'm just going out for drinks and chill at his place just for the night. I know you said you were going to move back home for awhile after Thanksgiving, and I just can't deal with that. I don't want you to go Caryn. I just hope that you can forgive me. Look, I'll call you later, I promise. We have to be at work in Norfolk at 7:00 tomorrow morning, so I will already be on this side of town. I love you Caryn." "I love you too," I replied.

After I hung up the phone, I sat there staring at myself for a long time in the mirror. My mind went back to the evening when Missy was here. "Caryn you are crazy if you stay with his ass! You think he's just fucking me? Hell no! I'm not the only one, trust me!" she had said. What did she mean by that? Is it possible there are other women too besides her?

112

You know old folks always say to don't go looking for things in your marriage. The truth is that looking may be what finally opens your eyes. I went and got our cell phone bills going back six months. Not only was Missy's number on there, but so where the numbers that Bernard had in his contact list as "K" and "S." Incoming, outgoing it didn't matter. They were regular calls for him. I decided to call "S" which was a long distance number to Maryland.

"Hello, this is Summer," a women's voice with a Caribbean accent answered. "Uh, Summer? I am calling because your phone number is showing up on our cell phone bill and I am not familiar with this number." She replied, "Our cell phone bill?" "Yes, my husband Bernard Williams. Your number seems to be everywhere." There was a pause on her end. "So, Bernard is not separated?" "No, he's not. How do you know him?" "Well if you are calling me, then I think you already know the answer to that question. Look, I don't want no mess, no drama. Please don't call my number anymore. Handle your business with your husband and leave me out of it," she said and hung up.

I sat there in a daze for a moment. I could feel my pressure rising. I pressed play on my VCR and watched today's episode of Young & the Restless. Genoa City, Wisconsin was where I went mentally for the next hour. Bernard called back around 11:00 that night and left a voice-mail saying that he was just checking in like he promised. "We just left this bar in Virginia Beach. We are on our way back to Kenny's now. I'm going to crash when I get there. I'll call you in the morning. Love you."

I listened to that message, and rolled over and watched the news until I dozed off. I woke up around 2:30. I had been dreaming that I had fallen in this deep hole and couldn't get out. It was cold and dark. I was screaming for help. I could see Bernard at the top, and he tried to pull me out. I kept reaching for his hand, but it wouldn't reach. I kept falling deeper and deeper into the hole. Finally, he grabbed me and started to pull me up. Then my hand slipped out of his and I fell even deeper. He couldn't help. He just couldn't help.

I woke up in a sweat. I laid there for an hour tossing and turning. Something about that dream, about my conversation with Summer, about everything just didn't seem right. I took off my nightgown, threw on a sweat suit and some sneakers and got in my car. I pulled up in Missy's apartment complex and rode around until I saw our truck. There it was. Bernard had lied again. He didn't stay over no co-worker's house, he was right here where he's been all along, right here with her. As I sat there, the song Silly came on and I listened, really listened to the lyrics: "You're just a love around to scold. I know that I should be looking for more. What could it be in you I see? What could it be? Silly of me..." How ironic I thought.

114

I called my Aunt Max because I really didn't know what to do at this point at 4:00 in the morning. "Caryn, do you want me to come up there and get you? Please don't do anything foolish!" "I'm such an idiot, I am such an idiot!" I kept saying over and over. Aunt Max replied, "Girl you are not an idiot, you are a woman that loved and trusted with her heart. He's the idiot! Come on over to my house, I'll be up," she said trying to get me to leave. "Ok," I said and hung up. I had notebook paper on the back seat. I wrote him a short letter and left it on the windshield. It read, "Here you go again. You ain't nothing but a mother fucking liar. You two deserve each other. I want you and your shit out of my house. I'm done. She can have your ass. Caryn." It was short but to the point. It wasn't much else to say really.

I sat there for a few more minutes. I thought about something that Mr. Washington had asked me in our last counseling session. "Can you live with the fact that, if you stay with your husband, that there will be times that he will not come home? Are you willing to share him?" Well, the answer to that question was no. I went home and packed enough clothes to last at least a week until I could get the rest of my things. My momma didn't raise no fool for real. I had done all that I could. I left him.

13

AFTER YOU'VE DONE ALL YOU CAN

I went to my Aunt Max's house. Bernard started calling me on my cell phone early that morning I guess as soon as he saw the letter. Missy called a couple of times too. My focus had shifted from "us" to "me" and what I needed to do next. I knew I needed to find a place to live in Richmond, sell the house here, and look into getting a lawyer. Those were the top three things on my list.

I finally answered my phone around noon. I guess Bernard was on a lunch break. "Caryn, what the fuck are you doing? What, now you're following me? And you calling numbers from my fucking cell phone? Is this what marriage is supposed to be like?"

he ranted. "Bernard you must have lost your damn mind! I am the victim here, not you. You are the liar, not me!" I yelled. "Well, uh you didn't even ask why I was there. You haven't given me a chance to explain," he said now sounding much softer. "Bernard, your girlfriend has already left me a message letting me know the real deal as she called it," I said.

Actually, her voicemail message was just another validation that I needed to get out of this mess ASAP. It said, "Ummm Caryn, Bernard told me that you left a note on the truck this morning. And the answer to the question is yes, he was here with me last night all night before you call me asking. Bernard and I have something special. I do think he cares for you, but I think he's just always needed you like for security or something like when he lost his job. Maybe it's your money? Anyway, I understand him, and I know what he needs. We are in love and ain't nothing going to keep us from being together. Can't nobody touch the passion that we have for each other. Sorry to have to tell you the real deal, but you need to know. From what Bernard tells me, you're a strong woman so you can handle it. Take care, and have a safe trip back home." She hung up on that note. I'm not sure what it was that she got out of leaving me that message, but she sounded like she had won the lottery or something. Missy may have gotten something, but it damn sure won't no fucking prize.

Bernard continued, "Well you can't believe Missy, she'll say anything." "I guess Summer is a liar too?"

"You know what Caryn? I am sick of all this. It's all out in the open now, now what? You want to leave me? Then go the hell back to Richmond," he yelled. "Bernard, you ain't nothing but a lying, cheating, broke ass bastard. I want you and your shit out of my house. All your bitches can help you move out for all I care! I am threw with your dumb ass!" I hung up before he could say anything. My knees fell to the floor, and the tears fell and fell and fell. This was some crazy shit here, just some wild shit. I spent the rest of the day talking to my Aunt Max crying, and trying to figure out my next step.

The next morning, we got up and went to Aunt Max's church like we normally did. I had to go this morning. I needed to be near God. I was ok during the service until the choir sang, "After you've done all you can, you just stand..." I lost it.

I had to go to work Monday morning because I had promised one of the professors that I would speak at his Business 101 class at 10:00. Luckily I had finished and printed my presentation before we left for the Thanksgiving break last week. The presentation went well and the students asked some very good questions. Working with the students can be so refreshing. Just so young and looking forward to their future.

I drove my car in this morning instead of taking the van because I wanted to start looking for apartments. I looked at two complexes after work.

One was perfect and they told me I could move in mid December. I felt like I was pretty productive today. I found an apartment, scheduled a meeting with a realtor for Saturday about selling the house, contacted a few moving companies, and re-scheduled my appointment with Mr. Washington for an earlier date. I was on a mission and functioning on pure adrenalin. I had five calls from Bernard today, but I didn't answer any of them.

I took off work Friday so that I could go by the house and get the rest of my clothes and do a little packing while Bernard was at work. I did not want to run into him. Aunt Max went with me. When I opened the door, the house looked a complete mess. It looked like a hurricane had hit it. Papers, bills, dishes, just stuff everywhere. I went upstairs to the bedroom, and it was even worse. It looked like he had thrown one of the dresser drawers against the wall. The wall was scratched and the drawer was on the floor and had a crack in it. He had dumped my lingerie and hosiery on the floor. He had cut up pictures of us and just thrown them all over the bed. The only thing my Aunt Max could say was, "Oh my God. Caryn, I think he lost it. Let's hurry up and get the hell out of here before he comes back."

The tears started falling again, but I knew that I had to focus. We were able to get all of my clothes and suitcases out and pack up a few things in the kitchen.

Saturday morning, Bernard called me and left me a message ranting and raving like some lunatic. "Caryn, I can't believe you sneaking in and out of the house like that trying to avoid me! What you can't even see me now? I've been trying to call you all week. You can't even talk to me? I don't even know where you are. Your Aunt Max won't talk to me either. Fuck it just fuck it!" then he hung up.

He called me right back and left me another message, "Caryn, please talk to me baby. I didn't mean those things I said to you. I don't want you to go. I don't want it to be over. Please just answer the phone."

I had an appointment with the realtor at 11:00. This was the same realtor that helped us find our house. They were surprised to see me because it had only been a little over a year since we'd bought it. "Mrs. Williams, what can we do for you today?" Lisa, the realtor asked. With tears in my eyes, I said, "Please just get me the hell out of that house." I sat there and cried right there at the conference room table.

I took off Monday so that I could try to undo some of the damage Bernard had done in the house and pack some more things while he was at work. My mom came down and Aunt Max helped too. I was able to move faster and get more done with them helping me. We finished around 2:00. I left a note telling Bernard that the house was going on the market and that he needed to get his things out.

By Thursday, the "for sale" sign was in the front yard. Bernard called me at work, my cell phone, my mother's house, Aunt Max's, everywhere he could think of. One of the messages he left on my cell phone was, "Caryn, you selling the house for real? Please don't do this. Please don't do this to us." To us? I would learn later with my sessions with Mr. Washington that this was and always has been Bernard's way of shifting the blame away from himself and inflicting it on me. A way to try to make me second guess my decision or to make me feel guilty. A form of control. Another message he left was, "I'm so sorry Caryn. I know I hurt you. But you know I love you, I love you with all my heart baby." I love you. Words that every woman wants to hear from the man she loves. He's always done that. That was his weapon. Another form of control and my weakness.

By mid December, the house had sold and I moved into my apartment. I had movers to move my things from Hampton to Richmond. My mom and Aunt Max helped too especially with trying to get the house cleaned. I had not seen or talked to Bernard even though he called and left messages daily. I communicated to him by leaving letters at the house. He even left me a couple of notes. They were pretty much the same, "I never meant to hurt you,"

"I never meant for this to happen," and "I hope you can one day forgive me."

The day I moved out of our house was very difficult. I looked around the place and just remembered how happy we were when we first moved in. We talked about having our babies and raising them right there. I asked the movers to wait outside while I locked up. I laid down on the living room floor all sprawled out and just cried like a baby; like a baby that just had its pacifier yanked out of its mouth.

After I got myself together, I got up and took one last walk through the house, room by room. The new owners would be moving in the first week of January. I wondered if they would find joy and peace in this house. How did we end up here? How did I let myself end up here?

Somehow I actually felt a sense of relief that first night in my apartment. I was back home in Richmond and I didn't have to deal with anymore drama. Is he coming home tonight? Is he with her? Is he lying? I didn't have to worry about any of that anymore. All I had to be concerned about was me, myself, and I.

I was exhausted mentally and physically after moving all day. After my mother left, I took a nice long bubble bath with my peppermint candles burning on the side of the tub. I hadn't felt this relaxed in a long time. Thank you God for delivering me out of there and for giving me the common sense to get the hell out. That was my prayer that night as I lay in my bed, my new home.

I worked right up until Christmas Eve. The students had gone home for the semester, and most of the employees had started taking off too. I kept busy during the day by working, evenings by working out at the gym, and nights by unpacking and getting my new apartment the way I wanted it to look. Bernard was still calling but not every day. Most of the time he would try to call me at work. I still had not actually talked to him since the day after I found him with Missy almost a month ago. I just couldn't talk to him. The whole thing was just too painful.

I did meet with Mr. Washington a couple of times though since I moved out. I kind of got the feeling that Mr. Washington was glad that I made the choice to leave Bernard. I know counselors are supposed to be neutral, but I felt like we had bonded a little and he was more like a big brother rather than a stuffy old counselor. My sessions with him were good though. He helped me to analyze and process the decisions and choices I'd made during the course of my relationship with Bernard. It basically came down to the fact that I had fallen in love with a man who couldn't commit and was addicted to sex. "You weren't the only woman in his life. There were and always have been other women. Some were important to him, some were not as important.

For those that were, such as yourself, he probably did love you all in his own way whatever way that was," is what Mr. Washington said in our session that evening December 23rd. Just what I needed to hear right here at the holidays. Depressing.

I couldn't get myself to get out of the bed Christmas morning. I cried off and on all day. My phone would ring but I just couldn't bring myself to answer it. The thought of hearing someone say, "Merry Christmas" made me cry. It was bad enough I kept hearing them say it on the local and national news. This was supposed to be our first Christmas as husband and wife, and what? I am here all alone feeling miserable. How in the world am I going to get through this holiday?

My family was gathering at my mom's house that evening. She called me I know three times that morning. My dad called probably five times. I finally called them both back around noon. "I'm not sure mom if I am going to come this evening. I just don't feel up to it. Can you just fix me a plate?" I had to assure and reassure my dad that I was fine and that he didn't have to worry about me. "Why don't you ride up here to Maryland if you don't want to go to your mom's? You shouldn't be alone today. Not on Christmas, Caryn," my dad said.

The truth is that I just wanted to be by myself. I hadn't taken anytime off since the move and had been pretty much busy up until now. I guess when

I finally was able to sit still, the whole reality of this whole mess just hit me all at once. It just happen to hit me on Christmas of all days.

I didn't go anywhere Christmas Day. I stayed in the bed and watched TV. I had a sandwich and pasta salad for dinner and lemon chess pie for desert. That was nothing compared to the feast that they were going to have at my mom's. I just would have to pass on the holiday fixings this year. My mother told everyone that I was sick, which was true in a sense. I was sick all right; sick of how my life had turned out.

My phone rang about 7:00 am the next morning. Monica had given birth to twin girls. I could hear them crying in the background. I was so excited for her. "Girl, you've gotta come see my babies. Call me once you book your flight!" she said before she hung up. I went on-line to see if I could find any deals. Before I knew it, I had booked my flight to Chicago for mid January.

Aunt Max came to visit New Year's Eve. She, my mom, and I went to church for watch night service. I must say on the one hand I was happy to say bye-bye to 2003. On the other hand, it was rather depressing to reflect on the roller coaster ride that this year had me on; a ride that ultimately ended in a head on collision. As I knelt on my knees while the preacher prayed us into 2004, I continued to thank God even in the midst of it all. The choir sang quietly in the background, "Before I ask for anything, I want to thank You for everything. Thank you. Thank you. Thank you Jesus; for all you've done for me….."

Service was good, and we had light refreshments afterwards. We then went back to my mom's for a glass of wine. "May 2004 bring us all that our hearts desire; and may God grant us peace and many many blessings!" Aunt Max prayed as we toasted our glasses.

Aunt Max and I got back to my place around 2:00 a.m. We were both exhausted. That morning I cooked breakfast and we talked until it was time for her to head back to Hampton. "I like what you've done to your apartment Caryn. You know I've been worried about you. But you know you're going to make it through this. You know that right?" "I know. I still can't believe it though Aunt Max. I'm supposed to be a newlywed now enjoying my first holiday with my husband. You know we've only been married three months, three freaking months. It's embarrassing, just embarrassing."

"Yes, the situation is unreal and messed up. But, you don't have anything to be embarrassed about. If anybody should be embarrassed, it's Bernard. He lied, he cheated, he messed up lives including his own. He's the one who has to face everybody with shame, not you my dear! Ok, well I'm going to get on the road and swing by the outlets for a little New Year's Day shopping on my way back. You sure you don't want to go with me? You could follow me down to Williamsburg?" "No, I'll pass this time. I may hit the mall here sometime today. You know shopping always makes me feel better," I said smiling. "Good to see that smile. There you go. There's my Caryn," she said giving me a big hug at the same time.

I did go out for a little while later that day. I bought a cute pantsuit and a pair of shoes. I went by my mom's house for dinner that evening. She had black-eyed peas, barbeque chicken, potato salad, and cabbage. Um, um, um. Ain't nothing like mama's cooking. I know folks say that black eyed peas are supposed to bring you good luck in the New Year, but I never did acquire a taste for them; they just didn't do anything for me. So, needless to say I pigged out on everything else! It was good too. I took a plate home for tomorrow's dinner so I wouldn't have to cook.

My cell phone rung about 10:00 that night. It was Bernard. I didn't answer, and he didn't leave a message. The last time he called was earlier in the week. He called me at work, but didn't leave a message then either. I wonder if his New Year's felt as jacked up as mine did. Oh well.

I couldn't wait until the next couple of weeks came and went. I left for Chicago that mid January on a Thursday evening for a long weekend stay with Monica. Her mom picked me up from the airport because Monica didn't want to bring the babies out.

They were only about three weeks old still; plus it was cold as shit. It was all of 15 degrees when I landed. I think all of my bones cracked from the bitter cold as soon as I stepped off the plane! My goodness, how do they stand it here?

Monica and her husband bought a new house I believe about two years ago. I hadn't been to the new house yet, so I was excited and couldn't wait to see it. When we pulled up in the long, winding driveway, my eyes opened as wide as a child's does on Christmas. The house was huge and absolutely gorgeous. The lawn was covered with snow, but I am sure it is even more beautiful in the spring; neatly and nicely manicured.

Monica and I gave each other the biggest and longest hug before I could even get in the house good. The house though was nothing compared to seeing those baby twin girls. When I saw them, my eyes teared up. They both had a head full of curly black hair, the tiniest hands and feet, and smelled like a mixture of freshly washed linen and baby powder! Too cute, just adorable. I think I held them both the whole afternoon. "Girl you are gonna spoil my babies. Put them down!" Monica said jokingly. "I can't put them down. I want one. I mean I want two!" I replied back.

Monica's mom showed me to the guest bedroom while Monica put the twins down for a nap. My room was more than spacious with a view looking out over their pool. It also had a full bathroom inside it which I loved. It was like a mini suite. While I was unpacking, Monica came in and said, "Let's go downstairs and each lunch. I am starving!" She had cooked this huge scrumptious Italian meal for us. "Girl, I got all your favorites. You know your mama should have named you Maria!" Monica said. We had manicotti, tossed salad, garlic bread, and spaghetti. It was so much that we had enough for dinner too.

We talked what seemed like for hours after lunch. Her husband was out of town on a business trip, so we had the whole weekend to ourselves. I never did quite figure out what he did for a living. Monica always said that he was an investor. Not sure what he invested in, but it damn sure seemed to be working for them especially with this five bedroom house. I didn't ask any questions though about his investment business. I had enough to worry about.

It was amazing watching Monica nurse the babies. I kept thinking about when we were in college and how long ago that now seemed. She was a mom, not just any mom but with twins! I never would have thought that she would start her family first. I always would have thought it would have been me. Funny how things turn out. It was meant to be though, because she was great with them. She was a natural, and made it look easy.

"I guess those big boobs of yours came in handy after all!" I said to Monica. "Ha, ha, ha! So tell me what's going on with you my friend," she responded. I had almost, and I mean almost, forgotten about my drama being here with her and the babies until she brought it up. By the time I had caught her up with everything, we both were on her sofa crying.

"He just couldn't leave her alone, he just wouldn't leave her alone. What's worse is that she wasn't the only one! And then after everything he had the nerve to be mad at me at tell me to go the hell back to Richmond! I feel like a complete fool Monica!" "Motherfucker. Ok, sorry to call your husband a mother fucker, but damn. Well, girl all I can tell you is that you had to do what was best for you. That's a bit much for anybody to take. I'm surprised you are still sane. I don't know if I could have handled it for real, Caryn. Sometimes I wonder what my man is doing, or should I say who he's doing, on his business trips because you just never know! I just try to believe in him because that's all we can do until we find out otherwise. And that's what you did. You gave him the benefit of the doubt based on what you thought you knew and what he led you to believe. Try not to blame yourself. You did it out of love Caryn; you loved him. So, now what?" she asked. "Well, I know I need to talk to him at some point. He keeps calling, but I just have not been able to bring myself to do it. All I want to do is just enjoy this weekend with you and those babies of yours!" As soon as I said that, the babies woke up crying almost on que. "Diaper changing time!" she said.

My weekend getaway to Chicago was what I needed. We didn't do too much on the outside because it was way too cold for me. I don't think the temperature got above that 15 degrees the whole time I was there. We did go out one night for dinner and drinks to a tapas bar. I spent as much time as I could with those little baby girls. I hated to say goodbye to them on Sunday.

Monica's mom came and watched the twins so that she could take me to the airport. "Well girl, hang in there and keep praying for strength. I'll be praying for you too. You know I am always here for you, always," she said. "I know. I'm happy for you. The baby girls are a blessing. I did pack one of them in my suitcase just in case you realize one is missing when you get back home!"

After going through all of the hustle and bustle of airline security, I didn't have much time before I had to board the plane. When I finally sat down on the plane, a sense of dread seemed to engulf me. Going back home meant going back to reality. Reality: what a bitch.

14

I WILL SURVIVE

The start of the new semester on campus is always pretty busy with a lot going on. I decided to go ahead and pursue my doctorate again. I had been taking a course here and there but had put it on hold over the last year. Having a doctorate was definitely a must have if I wanted that president position some day.

Not only did I go back to school, I joined another gym, and worked out on the evenings that I didn't have class. So my weekdays and evenings were pretty full. By the time I got home, ate dinner, and watched my soaps I was heading for bed.

The rest of January flew by. I still had not talked to Bernard even though he still continued to call me at work and on my cell phone. Most of the time though, he didn't leave a message. He would just hang up; sometimes after a long pause.

I dreaded going to work Valentine's Day. I just couldn't stomach all of the flower deliveries and all the talk about what everybody was doing for Valentine's Day and what their man gave them. I had requested the day off the first week of February because I just knew it would be too much. I treated myself to a massage and pedicure that morning and met Tammy for lunch. It took me a while to tell even her that I had left Bernard because the whole situation was still very embarrassing for me.

"Well girl how are you hanging in there?" "I'm doing, I'm doing. Doing a lot of praying!" I said. "Can I do anything for you? I feel like I should be doing something, I just don't know what." "Just being here is all I need. This is something I have to work out or figure out or whatever the hell by myself. Tell me what's happening with you," I said to hopefully change the subject.

Tammy went on to tell me about her new promotion. She was now a supervisor at the post office. She had worked hard there for years and was due for a promotion. "Well welcome to the world of management. It ain't easy and employees can work your last nerve!" I said and we both started laughing. "I have a thought. Why don't we go away to Jamaica for your birthday and take our moms? It can be our pre Mother's Day for them. We all need the break. What do you think?" "That sounds wonderful Tammy! You know we've been talking about going to Jamaica for years. Hell, let's do it!"

I didn't realize that I had cut my phone off, so when I went to check my messages I saw where Bernard had called me. As I began listening to the message, I heard music and then quickly recognized the lyrics: "This is straight from heart no one could ever doubt my love; will last till the end of time, of time..." "Straight from the Heart" was our song. I mean our song from when we first met in our 20's. He never said a word on my voice-mail; he just played that song, my song. There was a flutter in my heart, and the tears fell. Damn, he's good, damn.

He was so good that I did answer the phone when he called me a couple of days later. "Caryn, thank God you answered the phone! I've been trying to reach you for months. I was afraid that something may have happened to you. I'm, I'm so sorry for everything. Are you ok?" "What do you think Bernard?" "Did you get my voice-mail on Valentine's Day?" he asked, disregarding my question. "Yes," I responded curtly. "Look baby, look. We just need to get together and talk. I can make it up to you. I know I hurt you, but..." "But what Bernard? You did more than just hurt me. You made me feel like I did something wrong, like I wasn't enough, like I didn't or couldn't please you. You made me question myself, everything. I mean what was it that made you lie and cheat over and over again? All this time I thought it was about Missy, but there was Summer, and goodness knows who the hell else. The wedding, the whole relationship was a lie Bernard; one big joke. The sad thing is that the joke is and always has been on me though because everybody else was fucking clued in to the real deal; your family, even your women! Everybody knew, everybody except me. Then when all your dirt is finally out, you have the fucking nerve to tell me to go the hell back to Richmond? How could you do this to me? Why did you do this to me? All I ever did was love you and care for you. I gave you all of me. I didn't deserve this. This shit of yours got me in counseling! Counseling, counseling, what the fuck?" By this time, I am yelling and crying all at the same time. I may have started off calm, but somehow all of the rage that I had been holding in was coming out now full blast at his ass.

"Caryn, all I can tell you is that I never meant to hurt you and you didn't deserve this. You have been the one, the only one that has stood by me. You had my back when, when you should have left me a long time ago. I took your kindness and naiveness for granted, I admit it. I never thought you would leave me." "Are you still seeing Missy?" I asked him point blank. There was an awkward silence. "Are you still seeing her!!??" "Well Caryn, you left and I haven't talked to you. I mean you wouldn't talk to me and..." I stopped him. "I don't believe you. So after all of this, the break up, the house, everything, you are still messing around with her and it's my fault because I left you for lying and cheating in the first place? What is wrong with you? I hate you Bernard, I hate you! Just leave me the hell alone!"

I just fell to the floor and cried and cried and cried some more. As I lay in my bed that night, I wondered how many tears can a person cry before their eyes dried completely out. I had cried so much over the last few months, I just wondered how many more tears did I have left?

I cut the phone off last night and didn't turn it on until the next morning. I had a few hang-ups, so I assumed they were from Bernard. When I got to work, there was a voice-mail from him, "Ok, you hate me, you hate me, you hate me. Obviously I'm still hurting you. I got it. I won't bother you ever again," he said and hung up. I deleted that message and went on about my day which was booked solid. I had meetings all day, not to mention the fact that I had to prepare for class that evening. I never brought my personal mess into work. Once I got to work, my mind was all about my job and nothing else.

"So why do you think you reacted that way when you spoke to Bernard?" Mr. Washington asked in our counseling session a week later. "I don't know. I guess I was just so mad that he made it seem like it was my fault that he was still seeing Missy; my fault because I left him. I mean I'm confused. He left me that "Straight from the Heart" song message on my voice-mail Valentine's Day. It was, it was sweet, but then he's still seeing her too. I don't understand how somebody could do that. I just don't." "You don't understand it Caryn because it's not rational behavior. Your husband is not acting rationally. To try to figure out his actions would be impossible to do. You reacted the way you did because you are still grieving for the loss of him," Mr. Washington said. "What do mean grieving?" "Well people grieve separations and divorce similarly to how they grieve someone that has died. Anger, sadness, denial, etc. are all a part of the grieving process," he said.

Before I knew it, the session was over. I'd been going to Mr. fine ass Washington for almost six months now. I still ended up crying at some point each time at the sessions. Sometimes he'd piss me off with some of the questions he'd ask me. I guess he was trying to make me think, really think about the choices that I'd made these last thirteen years of my life. The more I thought about it, the madder I got with myself. How could I have been so stupid, so gullible? Why didn't I have sense enough to run for the hills way back in my 20's!! Look at the years, the time that I wasted. Now I'm almost 34 years old and what do I have to show for it? Separated, no kids, and a broken heart.

Bernard hadn't called in over a week thank goodness. Maybe he meant what he said last time, when he said he would never bother me again. So, now what? Is it over for real? I may not have heard from him, but I did have a couple of missed calls from Missy on my cell phone. Not sure what that was about, but I didn't call her back. I had been thinking about changing my cell phone number, but just hadn't gotten around to doing it. Now seems like the perfect time. My days of chatting with Miss Missy are done. I don't have shit to talk to her about. I got those 7 digits changed ASAP.

"Caryn, this is Bernard. So you changed your cell phone number? I guess you don't want me to reach you, huh? Well, I need to talk to you. It's important. Call me at work. It's an emergency." When I got to work, Bernard's message was the first one I heard. What is the emergency? I called my dad. "Should I call him back Daddy? I mean what's so important? What if it really is an emergency?" "All I can say baby girl is that if it really was an emergency he would have told you what the emergency was on the voice-mail. It's probably a ploy for you to call him back. But it's your choice if you want to call him back." My dad had a way of telling you what to do without making you feel like he just told you what to do.

Soon as I hung up with my dad, the phone rang. Bernard's work number was on the caller id. I didn't answer. He called again and again leaving two more messages, "Please call me Caryn. If you ever loved me, please call me. It's important." Ok, now I really don't know what to do. So I called Mr. Washington. "Oh Mr. Washington thank goodness, I caught you! Can you talk?" "Yes, Caryn, I am in between sessions, so I have a few minutes. What's up?" "Bernard keeps calling me leaving messages for me to call him saying that it's important and an emergency. He said if I ever loved him..." "Caryn, your husband is a smart man. You have changed the game. By changing your cell phone number, you have messed with his sense of security, his sense of control. Remember the cell phone bills where you saw how he would call his other women back to back when he couldn't reach them? It's his pattern Caryn."

"Ok, Mr. Washington can you just tell me what to do please??!!" I hate it when he gets all psychological on me; just tell me what the hell to do! Isn't that what I'm paying him for? "Now you know I can't do that. Think about what I just told you about the pattern. Think about your old habits and choices," he said. "I know, I know but he said, if I ever loved him which makes me think that it really is something wrong," I said. "Caryn, think about what we've talked about in our sessions and how and when your husband chooses to use the word love. You shared with me that many times he chooses to use it when he has done something wrong and needs your forgiveness. I can't tell you what to do. I can only make you open your eyes and help you to see for yourself." Although I didn't want to hear it, Mr. Washington was right. I can't get sucked back in. Whatever Bernard's emergency is, Missy can take care of it dammit.

By April, Tammy and I were all set for our trip to Jamaica with our mothers. I was ready to go too.

I had pretty much put my so called marriage out of my head for awhile at least. I'm not sure whatever happened with Bernard's "emergency," but he stopped calling for about two weeks before he started calling me again. I would still get hang-ups on my work phone. Most of the time they were blocked calls or from pay phones. He hadn't left any messages though, and that was fine with me.

We left for Jamaica mid-April, my birthday weekend. We had an early flight departing Friday morning, and were in sunny Jamaica by noon. This was our first time visiting Jamaica, so we were all real excited. I was just glad to be away in such a beautiful paradise for my birthday.

When we arrived at our all inclusive resort, we were greeted by two shirtless, tall, handsome Jamaican men. "Welcome to Jamaica beautiful ladies," they said in their sexy native accents handing us all glasses of rum punch. "Ok, are ya'll blushing?" I said to my mom and Tammy's mom. They just giggled like little horny teenagers. "Can't take you two nowhere!" Tammy said.

We spent most of the weekend relaxing on the sandy beach. We did do some shopping at the markets, and we did water aerobics every day at the resort. We went out on my birthday into town for dinner and drinks. The food was delicious: jerk chicken, plantains, and beans and rice was my birthday choice. A few native men came over and tried to flirt with us. Jamaican men tickle me because they act like we American women are the best thing around since slice bread. Charming and seductive is probably the best way to describe them. Unfortunately for them, my "groove" was on lockdown and I wasn't trying to get it back, not just yet.

Sunday was our last day, so we all slept in late that morning and took our time getting up and dressed. After eating a huge buffet brunch, we went out on the beach and laid out for a few hours. Later that evening, one of the guys that we met the night before took us on a private tour of the island on his tour bus. He took us to see the homes of the Jamaican elite, and to a local spot where you could see the sun setting over the ocean. It's hard to describe it, but it was just gorgeous. I don't think you've witnessed a true sunset until you've seen it set in Jamaica.

That night we laid out by the pool and just enjoyed feeling the ocean breeze. This weekend was what the doctor ordered. Nobody mentioned anything about the drama in our lives the whole time we were there. Everything we talked about was uplifting, positive, and spiritual. I needed to be away for my birthday and I couldn't have asked for a better way to bring in age 34.

I went back to work Tuesday to 50+ e-mails and at least 10 voice-mails. One of the messages was from Bernard, the day after my birthday. "Hey Caryn, I hope you had a nice birthday. I, I hope that you are ok," he said and hung up. The caller id showed that he had called a couple of times yesterday and Monday, but he didn't leave any more messages. The phone rang just as I had finished checking my messages. It was Bernard. I didn't answer it, and he didn't leave a message. Goodbye Jamaica; hello reality.

Before I knew it, that summer had come and gone. It was a good one though. I went to Maryland a couple of times to visit family, took a weekend bus trip to New York to see a Broadway play, went to a few outdoor concerts, took one doctoral course, and just spent as much time as I could trying to enjoy each God given day.

Although I did my best to keep busy, my heart still ached and there were many nights where I cried myself to sleep. I continued to work out. Not only did it help me to keep it tight (a girl's always gotta look good), but it was the one way I could let out all the stress that was still bottled up inside.

That next October seemed to come by way too fast. I hadn't talked to Bernard in nearly 8 months. He kept up his routine though by calling me at work. He would call and either hang up or leave a message. Some days I would have 3 or 4 hang-ups from him. It was hard to believe that we got married a year ago this month.

On the morning of our one year anniversary, I called in sick. I thought I could be a big girl and go into work and not think about it, but that was further from the truth. I couldn't handle being at work today. I had been up and in the bathroom all night. I know it was just my nerves. I decided to forgo work and just go to the appointment with Mr. Washington I had scheduled for 1:30. I did manage to squeeze in a massage appointment at 3:00.

One whole year. I was supposed to be happy today. We were supposed to be celebrating a year of wedded bliss. I was supposed to still be a blushing newlywed. Damn, I am supposed to be having good morning wake up sex with my husband right now. The more I thought about it, the madder I got. Sometimes I don't know if I should be mad or sad. Most times I'm both. Right now, I'm mad.

"So, how are you today, Caryn?" Mr. Washington asked as I sat down on the lounging chair in his office. "Pissed. More like mad as hell!" "I know what today is, and I can only imagine how you feel. Tell me what's going on," he said. "I still can't believe all of this. It's like one minute I think I'm dealing with it and handling my business. The next minute, I'm crying and on my knees. Right now, I just I just can't believe it. I don't know what else to say." A tear fell down my cheek, and he pushed that damn box of tissues over closer to me. "I'm tired of crying, I'm tired of not knowing what to do, I'm tired of coming here seeing you. No offense." "None taken," he said not seeming offended. "I just thought he loved me. I always thought he loved me even when things were funky. How could he do this to me? What am I supposed to do now? Divorce him, file for legal separation, what?" I asked, the tears streaming down my face. "Well you certainly do not have to make any decisions now if you are not ready. You still have unresolved feelings, Caryn. At some point though, you will have to think about your next step."

Before I knew it, our hour was up. "Remember the best relationship is one in which your love for each other exceeds your need for each other," Mr. Washington said. I thought about that statement while I laid on the massage table an hour later. The best relationship is one in which your love for each other exceeds your need for each other. The truth is that Bernard had always needed me from the day we met. All these years, I had been his emotional and financial safety net, his alibi, his meal ticket, the roof over his head. How could I have been so blind? I had always thought that he was the love of my life. The truth is that I was never his.

That night, I watched the video of our wedding. I hadn't seen it since right after the wedding a year ago. As I watched it, I could feel the emotions that I had on my wedding day. I was so happy. We looked happy. The truth is that Bernard was carrying his deep dark secret that day. Even with all that had to be going on in his head with being with Missy the night before, knowing that she was trying to get to me to tell me everything so I would stop the wedding, the lies, the deception, his feelings for her... with all that going on, he still walked and talked with confidence and paraded around like this was his day too. Or was it all a façade? Maybe he was the one who wanted to break it off with me but went through with it anyway. Who the hell knows? All I know is that he carried it well.

I slept pretty good that night considering all of the crying and emotional mess I dealt with that day. Thank goodness, I made it through my anniversary. One day at a time, just one day at a time.

The next day at work, the receptionist called me and said, "You have a phone call from your husband. He said that he's having a hard time getting through. He says it was important, so I told him that I would stay on the line to make sure it goes through this time." Before I could blow a gasket, the phone was ringing. I had to answer it because if I didn't, she'd know that something was up. I didn't want to put my business out there and start the gossip going, so I was forced to take his call. Damn. Checkmate.

"Mr. Williams, your wife's on the line," the receptionist said and hung up. Bernard started, "Caryn, we have got to talk. It's been months. You won't answer none of my calls, so this was the only way I could get through." "By lying? What you do best," I responded sharply. "All righty. Sounds like you are still mad. Can you at least tell me how you are doing?" "I'm fine. I'll survive," I responded. "You miss me?" I didn't answer. "Well, baby I miss you.

I need you. Shit just ain't right. Nothing has been right since you left me. Everything is shot to shit!" "Are you still seeing Missy?" I asked. Long pause. He responded, "Uhm, Caryn I am not going to lie to you anymore. We are still friends, but..." "Then nothing has changed!" I said and slammed the phone down.

15

SPEAK TO MY HEART LORD

By the next week, I had scheduled an appointment with one of my college classmates who was a divorce attorney. When I arrived to the downtown office, this man walked up to me and said, "Hey pretty lady. Yo fine ass shouldn't be alone, where yo man at?" I don't know if he was homeless or what, but I wasn't in the mood to be hit on. I forced a half smile and kept walking. He then said, "My name Bernard sugar, what's yo name?" Sugar, who the hell uses the word sugar anymore? When I heard him say Bernard, I did a double take. Of all the names in the world, this man's name just happened to be Bernard. Was this some kind of sick sign? Was I doing the right thing?

I went on in the law office and filled out the necessary paperwork. I told the quick and dirty version of my story and the reason why I was filing for divorce. My attorney basically told me that our case should be pretty simple, no kids, no property. I knew what she meant by simple, but there was nothing simple about this to me. Nothing simple at all.

Bernard received his divorce documents a few days later. Since I didn't have a home address for him, they sent the papers to his job. I think as soon as he got those documents he called me. I was still at work, but I didn't answer the phone. He called me three times back to back, two messages and one hang up: "Caryn, how could you do this? You hate me that much that you gonna do this shit to me at work and embarrass me like this? All right, you want to play dirty. Fine. Fuck you Caryn," and he hung up. Then he called right back, "Caryn. Pick up the phone please. Why couldn't you have just told me that you wanted to end it? This ain't right. We can't end it like this. I know I hurt you, and I wish I could take it all back. I can't believe it has come to this. Please call me back Caryn, please. Don't do this!" he said and finally hung up.

He continued to call and hang up for about a week. One Friday, I was about to leave work for lunch and the receptionist called me and told me that I had a visitor. When I asked her who, she said, "Your husband." My heart stopped for like a minute.

I couldn't believe that he was here. I hadn't seen him in almost a year, I just couldn't believe he was here. What do I do? Should I tell the receptionist to tell him I'm not in, not available? Damn, damn! I decided to call Mr. Washington and ask him what the hell I should do. "You said you needed closure, Caryn. You said you needed answers. He's here to see you so sounds like he's stepping up the game a little bit. Just be careful. I don't believe that he would ever physically hurt you, but people do crazy things when they are desperate and feel like they are backed into a corner. Let me know how it goes."

I walked out to the reception area, and there he was. He looked tired and weary, but handsome just the same. I motioned for him to come on back and follow me to my office. He came in, sat down, and I shut the door behind him. "What are you doing here Bernard?" "You won't answer my calls, you won't talk to me, I had to come. I had no choice. I can't accept that it's over, not like this. I love you, I miss you, and I need you. I came here to tell you that I have ended it with Missy, and I have started going to counseling. I've only been to two sessions, but I have started going. I ain't gonna lie, its rough spilling my guts to a stranger, but you asked me to do it months ago. I'm doing it for you, for us."

I was actually pretty stunned listening to him, but I remained cool and unnerved looking. "Why should I believe that you are in counseling all of a sudden? And if you are, then you need to do it for yourself, not for me." "I knew you weren't going to believe me. Here's her business card and number. I have given her my authorization to speak to you. As for Missy, you have her number if you want to check with her. It's over this time. I know I've said it before but the stakes are just too high now. I am a fool if I fuck up what I have with you. Fourteen years man, I can't fuck it up. Not again," he said.

Bernard stayed for about thirty minutes doing most of the talking. He asked to take me to lunch, but I told him I had plans. "Well, I guess I'd better get back on the road. If you've ever doubted anything about me, never doubt that I love you and always have. I guess I just didn't know how to show it. Don't give up on me, us, not yet. Please call my therapist and talk to her." After he left, all I could say was damn. Checkmate. My move.

"Girl, get out! Bernard is seeing a therapist?" Tammy asked as she poured me a glass of white wine at her place that evening. "Yep, that's what he said. "His ass is serious sounds like, you think?" "I don't know, Tammy. I just don't know."

Tammy and I spent the rest of the evening eating pizza and finishing up that bottle of wine. We watched a couple of Lifetime Channel movies, and then I headed back home. I had a lot of studying to do. This semester was almost up, and working on this doctorate was not getting any easier.

I looked at that business card Bernard gave me I know ten times on Monday. Should I call? No, I shouldn't call. Shit, what the hell? I dialed the number. "Hello, I'm calling to see if you have a client named Bernard Williams?" A woman with an accent replied, "Who am I speaking to? We do not give out client information." "This is his wife Caryn Williams." I thought to myself I just know this was just another one of his lies. These folks don't know who the hell he is! "Yes, hello Caryn. I am Dr. Lopez. Bernard is my client, and he was adamant that I speak to you if you contacted me. How can I help you?" I think I fell faint for a second out of pure shock. "Uhmm, well how long has he been going to you, and what has he told you?"

"Bernard and I have had two sessions. He pretty much told me about you all's history and how you all got to where you are now." "So you know about the wedding, the women, the lies?" "I only know to the extent of what he has shared with me, and that he feels deeply bothered and guilty about what happened to you." I went on and gave her my version of the story so that she would have all the facts just in case his ass left out something. "This is good to know Caryn, thank you for sharing." I had other questions, but Dr. Lopez told me she couldn't divulge anything else. All she said was, "Bernard and I have another appointment scheduled for next week. It has been very hard for him to open up to a stranger, so I hope that he will continue his treatment with me. It was nice speaking with you. Please contact me anytime," she said and hung up. A part of me was glad that Bernard had started counseling, but the other part of me was a bit skeptical.

Before we knew it, the holidays had come around once again. I hadn't talked to Bernard since he'd come to visit my job a few weeks ago. He called around the first week of December asking if we could spend some time together "just to talk" during the holidays. "Did you talk to Dr. Lopez?" he asked. "Yes, I talked to her," I responded. "I'm trying baby, I swear to God I'm trying. I went to visit my dad last weekend, and we had a long talk. Funny how both of our lives is fucked up right now. He ain't been right since the divorce. Two marriages he fucked up; I don't want to be like him, Caryn. I've got to make it right. I've got too." I really didn't say anything because I just really didn't know what to say to be honest. I just listened and added an "uh huh, ok, yeah" whenever a response from me was warranted. "I have a couple of days off during Christmas and New Year's. Are you going to church New Year's Eve?" "Probably. You know I try to go every year," I responded. "Ok, I want to come with you. Can I Caryn?" "Bernard, I don't know. I, I, just let me think about it. I need to go now." There was a pause. "Well I didn't mean to hold you. I just wanted to hear your voice Caryn, and ask about New Year's. I love you," he said and hung up.

My mom hosted her annual Christmas Dinner at her house. It could barely hold the 50+ family members, but we made it work. Monica came with her husband and twin girls. The twins were so adorable. Just holding them made me feel that little "I want one" kind of twinge. Just looking at all of my family with their husbands, wives, boyfriends, children, whatever made me feel sad. Here goes the second Christmas without my husband. Maybe if things had worked out, we'd be here now with our baby or at least expecting our baby. I tried to hold back the tears. Aunt Max saw me and asked, "You ok, Caryn?" "Yeah, I'm ok," I lied.

Bernard caught me right as I was wrapping up at work for the New Year's break. I started not to answer the phone, but I did. "Happy Holidays Caryn." "Thanks, you too. Bernard, I am really busy right now. I am off until after New Year's, so I am trying to finish up a few things here," I replied hoping that he would just say ok. "I'm not going to hold you. I've just been thinking about you and well I still want to go with you to church tomorrow night for New Year's Eve. Can I do that, please?" I'm thinking Lord, what do I say? "I can't stop you from going to church Bernard," was all I could think to say. "Ok, I'll be there. See you tomorrow," he said and hung up. A bit in a daze, I finished up and did what I needed to do at my desk and then headed for my hair appointment.

"Daddy, Bernard wants to meet me at church tomorrow. Is it a trick or what?" I asked my dad on the phone that night. "Could be baby girl. A player has always got a trick or two up his sleeve. I don't know. All I do know is that you need to be careful and don't read into anything." After giving it some thought, I figured Bernard probably wouldn't show up no way. That was and has always been his MO. I just put it out of my mind.

Tammy, her mom, my mom, and I met at church the next evening around 9:40 so that we could get good seats. I didn't even mention to Tammy that Bernard said he may come. Church on New Year's of all nights? Nope, not him.

At around 9:55, I saw Bernard walking around the church looking for me. He had on a nice lavender button down shirt with a lavender/grey print tie, grey slacks, and a black leather jacket. He had a bit of the salt and pepper thing going on with his goatee and beard. Damn he looked good. I almost forgot that I hadn't too long ago served his ass divorce papers.

He spotted us, and came over to where we were sitting and sat in the pew in front of us. My mom looked at me as if to say "what the fuck?" but luckily she couldn't say it because we were like still in church. Tammy whispered, "Did you know he was coming?" I just shook my head like "girl, I don't know."

Right before midnight, the pastor had the congregation to get down on our knees while he prayed us into the New Year. "... And Lord we ask that you will bless each and every one of us here tonight with a new year full of joy, hope, and prosperity. We give you all the glory, in Jesus Name we pray Amen." It was the year 2005.

After church, Bernard walked us out to our cars. "All righty, well your momma still hates me. She wouldn't even look at me except for when she rolled her eyes!" I didn't say anything. "Well, I enjoyed church. It wasn't bad as I thought," he said and winked at me. I couldn't help but smile. "You didn't think I was going to come did you?" "Nope I sure didn't," I replied. "Well, I guess I'll get back on the road. Thanks for allowing me to come. Please don't give up on me Caryn, not yet."

Bernard continued to call me over the next few weeks at work. The divorce proceedings were still pending, and he wanted to know if we could meet to talk. He drove to Richmond one Saturday afternoon in late January. We had gotten a couple of inches of snow the day before, and it was cold as hell. We met at a restaurant around 1:00 for lunch. "Caryn, I ain't going to bullshit you. I miss you, and I don't want to get divorced. I want you, I need you back. What can I do? It's been over with Missy for months. I ain't been with nobody, nobody Caryn. I gotta make this right. I'll move up here if I have too. Say something please."

"Bernard, so much has happened. To be perfectly honest, I don't trust you and don't know if I could ever trust you again. The thought of getting back together with you and you hurting me again scares the hell out of me. I don't know if my heart can take being broken again not like that. Thank God I made it through this time, but what if I can't make it through the next time? What would happen to me then?" "Look baby, there will be no next time. I swear on my mamma's grave. My hurting you has been, I mean... my life, my soul ain't been right since... since I hurt you. There's no way I can leave this earth without righting that wrong. Of all the shit, I've ever done in my life, breaking your heart was the worst."

We talked for over three hours. The lunch crowd had gone, and the dinner crowd was beginning to trickle in. "I can't deal with this anymore right now," I said and got up from the table. "Well can I at least have your phone number so I can keep in contact with you?" I gave him my cell phone number so at least he would stop calling me at work, and it would shut him up for now anyway.

That night as I lay in bed, so many thoughts and images of our history flooded my mind. It had been over a year since I left my home, my life, my husband. Images of all the lies, the deception, the pain... I thought about the week after hurricane Isabel when Bernard left me home by myself: no electricity, no food, no hot water. Those lonely, dark nights where my only source of light was a candle and a flashlight. He let me think that he was working those nights, but he was with her; taking care of her and her family while letting me fend for myself.

I thought about meeting Missy and all that she so proudly and boldly told me: the years that they spent together, the sex tapes, the baby they lost... I thought about how happy I was coming back from our beautiful destination wedding and hearing her voice on our voicemail telling me all about her relationship with Bernard. I thought about how I threw up in that airport after listening to Missy's message and how my life and all of my dreams changed overnight.

But I also thought about how hard he has pursued me since the day I left him, never giving up; the fact that he had started counseling all on his own, how sincere and determined he now sounds and wanting to make things right with us. I thought about the good times, the day we first met, the laughter, making love, and dreaming together. There was this gnawing void in my life. I had suppressed it over the last year not even realizing it until now.

This is crazy! I would be a complete fool to go back to Bernard after all the shit he did! But doesn't God say that we should forgive? What if the separation was truly a wake-up call for Bernard? Should I give him one last chance? For better or for worse; isn't that what we promised each other? Speak to my heart Lord, please speak to my heart.

16

I STILL BELIEVE

I had nearly forgotten about the assignment that was due for my doctoral class I had on Tuesday. After turning that in, I decided to see if Mr. Washington could fit me in for a counseling session. We were pretty much doing only once a month sessions now, but I really needed to talk to him about my visit with Bernard. Oh good, he can see me at 4:30 tomorrow.

"So what's going on Ms. Caryn? What's happened now?" Mr. Washington asked with that Denzel looking smile of his. "Ok, so I don't know what to do!" I said and the tears started to fall one by one. "Caryn, tell me what it is and how you are feeling," he said now in professional mode. "I mean, he just won't give up. He wants me to give him like chance number 350!" The tears were still trickling down my face and my voice was cracking big time. "And what are you feeling?" I paused and then responded, "I'm confused. I don't know if I can believe him or trust him. He's in counseling and he's coming at me just as hard as he has all these months, but it just feels different. Should I, should I forgive him?" Now I am crying even harder. Damn PMS. "What do you mean different?" he asked. "Sincere, like it's coming from his heart this time. No games, no schemes, it seems real. And that scares the hell out of me."

I looked at my watch. Our hour was almost up. He gave me a lot to think about. Finally I said, "Ok Mr. Washington could you please just tell me what the hell to do?" He smiled and told me that it was ultimately my decision, and that nobody could tell me what to do. "Remember I told you a long time ago, "The best relationship is one in which your love for each other exceeds your need for each other."

That night after watching the video of our wedding and two glasses of wine later, I was like shit I can't do this. I've got to move on. Too much has happened. Like my dad said, I would never truly trust Bernard again.

So, when Bernard called me the next day I told him that we needed to meet again. He came to Richmond the following Saturday. I figured once I talk to him this last time, then I could put it all behind me and I can focus on me, like finishing up my doctorate for one. Finding a man would be two.

When Bernard got to my house, he walked around and said, "Very nice Caryn. I wouldn't have expected anything less." "Well, this has been my sanctuary. I like it. It's home." We talked for awhile and then Bernard pulled me to him and said, "Ok, Caryn what's it going to be? Will you give me, us, this marriage another chance?" He looked me dead in my eyes seemingly right to my soul. I had mentally and emotionally prepared for this last conversation all week. I knew exactly what I was going to say, but God help me, the history, the pull was too strong. He leaned over and kissed me gently and my body went limp. "I love you Caryn, I need you Caryn, he said over and over. The old feelings, the rhythm, everything swooped over me like flashes of lighting. I could feel the heat coming from the both of us. We moved and swayed and rocked and grinded like a favorite song that you hadn't heard in way too long. I felt his hand, his fingers move down between my thighs and the feelings and memories came rushing back. He looked at me as if to ask me if it was ok, but he knew the answer. We both knew the answer. We were lost in the moment, and the tears of joy, fear, ecstasy fell.

I missed him. Lying in his arms again felt good, I must admit it. We talked about how what we'd been through and what we wanted to do from here. I wish I could say that this was just a booty call for me, but it was much more than that. Lord knows I've been hornier than a freaking nun, but that was only a small part of it.

"Tell me what I need to do Caryn to try to make this marriage work and fix the damage that I've done." "Well I'm not moving down there ever again. I'm done with Tidewater, so I don't know," I responded. "I guess I'll have to move here then. Richmond it is," he said smiling. "But your job is in Hampton. What are you going to do about work?" "I'll just have to commute it until I can find a job up here. Baby, I don't have no choice."

The next morning after breakfast, he left. I called my Aunt Max. "Ok, so I slept with my husband," I said when she answered the phone. "Oh-k," she said slowly and hesitantly. "Just be careful baby and go with your brain and not so much your heart. We've all been there. We take them back, we always take them back." Talking to my Aunt Max always made me feel better. After I hung up with her, I decided to start studying for an exam I had this week. I'd damn near forgot about trying to finish up my doctorate.

Bernard and I "dated" over the next few weeks; talking on the phone every day, and seeing each other every weekend. By the end of March we'd decided that he would go ahead and move into my place. I made my fears and my expectations perfectly clear. He said he heard me, but I pray to God that he really really heard me.

Of course I had to go see Mr. Washington to let him know the latest developments. I'm not 100% sure, but I got the feeling that he was a bit disappointed about my decision to reconcile with Bernard. Mr. Washington had become like a big brother or a cool uncle to me versus my therapist. He gave me his professional advice but he also would throw in his personal advice too. "Well, you know where to find me if you need me. Try to encourage your husband to continue his therapy too. I'm here if you need me," he said as I left his office.

By early April, Bernard had moved to Richmond and was commuting daily to Tidewater to work. My mother was livid when I told her. "Girl, I told you once a dog, always a dog! Caryn, he's going to hurt you again, I'm telling you. God has someone else out there for you who will love you the way you deserve to be loved. If it were me, I'd run as far away as I could," my mama told me. My father, I guess being a man, wasn't as harsh with his words as she was. "It is going to be hard for you to truly trust him and you both are going to have to work really hard to make it work. The odds are against you sweetheart, the odds are against you."

All righty then. Words of wisdom from your parents. Gotta love them. Bless their hearts, they continue to try to protect you even when you are growner than grown, but ultimately the decisions we make as adults are our own, and I made the decision to give my husband another chance. I still believed in us and wanted to give it another shot.

It was a bit weird having Bernard back in my life, my home, in my bed after everything we'd been through and after so much time had passed. He did that commute back and forth between Hampton and Richmond, but it was rough. One night he decided to spend the night at Jay's instead of driving back home to Richmond. Before he left that morning, he kissed me and said, "I know you still don't trust me. I promise you that I will be at Jay's place and nowhere and with nobody else."

He called me when he got to Jay's after work, then called me a couple of times from there up until he went to bed. He then called me first thing in the morning from Jay's. "I just want to show you that you can trust me, and I am trying." It was a bit comforting, but there was still a part of me wondering if he was with Missy.

We decided to spend my birthday weekend at the beach. I loved the month of April, not just because it was my birthday month but because the weather starts to get warm, the flowers bloom, and it's just the perfect time of year. I actually could not remember a better birthday spent with Bernard than this one. We walked along the beach, talked, and made love until the wee hours of the morning. He gave me one single red rose and told me he loved me and he would spend the rest of his life proving it to me.

After a few weeks, I contacted my attorney and told her that Bernard and I had reconciled and that I wanted to hold on the divorce proceedings. I also finished up the Spring semester with my doctoral classes. With Bernard being here with me, I decided to not take any summer courses so that I could focus my attention on my marriage.

Memorial Day came before we knew it. We decided to lay low and not do the family cookout thing because neither one of us were ready for the drama. Although I had forgiven him, nobody else either in his family or mine had. I just wasn't in the mood for no confusion. We cooked out on the grill and invited Jay and Tammy. Whatever thing those two had going on back in St. Thomas when we got married still seemed to be there. We had a nice time eating, drinking, and playing cards. For once in a very long time, we felt like a real married couple.

The July 4th holiday seemed to come just as fast as Memorial Day did. Bernard called me at work and asked me what I wanted to do that holiday weekend. He said he wanted to go to Maryland to his uncle's cookout. He really had not had much dealings with his family or most of his friends either for that matter since our separation. "Just too embarrassing, and I needed to focus on getting myself right for you, for us," he said. I wasn't very excited about seeing his family after all that Missy had told me about her little visits to his family get togethers and shit over the years. They all knew about her, but nobody cared to clue me in. But, if I am going to give this marriage another shot, then I knew I would have to try or at least put on a damn good front with my in-laws. "Ok, well while we're in Maryland, we're going to visit my father too." "Caryn, I'm not ready for that yet. I can't face him with all that I've done to you. It ain't right, the timing ain't right. By the holidays though, I promise I'll be ready to face him."

That next Sunday, Bernard went with me to my church. I must admit the sermon was inspiring and on point. The reverend talked about forgiveness; how we hold on to past hurts, pains, disappointments. It was truly fitting for Bernard and me because, although I had forgiven him, he still had not forgiven himself. He had been carrying that guilt for over a year, and it still pained him. "I like that preacher. He's pretty cool. I can see myself joining this church," Bernard told me after the Sunday service. "Are you serious?" I asked. "Yep, I really could," he said and smiled. I thought to myself, wow. I never would have imagined we would get here to this place. God knows this man needs Jesus! His joining church and us worshiping together would be one more step in the right direction.

Later that night, we sat up and talked for a long time. "Caryn, do you forgive me, really?" I pulled out the letter from my attorney's office stating that I was no longer retaining them and pursuing the divorce proceedings and handed it to him. A tear fell down his cheek. "Does that answer your question?" I asked grabbing hold to his hand.

We made love that night, and for the first time we felt like husband and wife. No outside influences, no drama, just hope for our future. And no protection... "Bernard, you know we didn't use any protection, so you know what that means?" I asked playfully. "I've always wanted you to have my babies, Caryn; that ain't changed. If you get pregnant, we'll just name the baby Oopsie," he said with a wicked smile as he dozed off to sleep.

The next morning Bernard kissed me and said see you later as he left at 5:00 that morning to head to work. He had put in a few applications here in Richmond, so we were hoping he would find a job here soon and wouldn't have to commute anymore.

I lay there for awhile but couldn't go back to sleep. I thought about the last couple of years and how Bernard and I ended up here. We had a lot that we were both still dealing with. I'd forgiven him, but I damn sure hadn't forgotten. Man, what if I did get pregnant last night? What if things don't work out? What if this is all just too good to be true?

I finally got on up and decided to walk a quick mile around the block to get some exercise in. Work was pretty uneventful that day. Summer session was in, so the campus was in full bloom with student enrollment and summer activities. I decided to leave a little early so I could get home and start cooking by the time Bernard got home. "Damn, I've missed home cookin since you left me!" he'd been saying since we've been back together. I found a sexy nightgown that I decided to change into so it would be the first thing he saw when he walked in the door. I figured I would do my wifely duties figuratively and literally this evening!

I was on my way home from work around 4:30 when my cell phone rang. I figured it was Bernard because the area code on the caller id was from Hampton. "Is this Caryn?" the woman asked when I answered. I immediately started thinking oh God not again, not again. "Who is this?" I asked with as about as much restraint that I had. "This is Dr. Juanita Russell from Hampton General Hospital. I am calling about a Bernard Williams. Your number was the last number dialed on his cell phone. What is your relationship to Mr. Williams?" "This is his wife, what's wrong?" "You are his wife?" "Yes!" I said now with a bit of panic. "Well, Ms. Williams your husband has collapsed, and we are trying to revive him. How soon can you get here?" "Well uh, uh I am in Richmond, but I can get there. It might be over an hour, but I am right near the interstate now. Is he, ok?" "Just get here as soon as you can. I will fill you in then. Tell me, how old is your husband?" "Thirty nine," I said. "Ok, I'll see you when you get here. Drive safely."

Sheer panic is what I felt. I called Tammy and my mother to let them know what was going on. My mom said, "Ok he's unconscious so that means he still has a chance, so just talk to him. I truly believe that he will be able to hear you. Just talk to him. Let me ride down there with you Caryn." "I can't wait mom, I am already on the interstate. I have to get to him. I'll call you once I know something." After I hung up with her, Tammy called me back and told me that she was leaving work and was picking my mother up in about 30 minutes and they would head on down to Hampton and meet me.

In all of the confusion, I realized that I hadn't called Bernard's father. When I did, he told me he would be leaving and heading down too. It would be an almost three hour ride for him from Maryland. He called me back about 15 minutes later and told me that he and his brother were getting ready to leave then. My mind was in a blur. What in the world happened? Was he going to be ok? My nerves were so rattled, my stomach was churning. Dammit, I gotta go to the bathroom. Of all times, I had to take a damn shit! I couldn't hold it, I felt like I was going to explode. So, I pulled into a rest stop.

When I got back in the car, my Aunt Max called. I had forgotten all about calling her. "Hey girl, your mom told me what happened. Where are you?" "Aunt Max I don't know what happened to him and my stomach is a mess. I had to go to the damn bathroom. But I'm about 20 minutes away now,"

I said trying to be calm. "It's your nerves that's all. Just call me when you get to the hospital. I am going to show your mom and Tammy how to get there. We'll all meet you, ok? Hang in there girl."

That one hour and twenty minute drive seemed like forever. When I finally pulled into emergency, my phone rang. It was Bernard's father. "Are you there yet? Me, and my brother and sister are on the way." "Yes, I just parked and about to walk in the hospital now. I'll call you once I know something more." When I walked up to the emergency window and told the lady who I was and who I was looking for, she immediately said, "Yes, Ms. Williams we've been waiting for you. Someone will be with you shortly, please have a seat." In a few short minutes, the chaplain walked up to me and introduced herself and asked that I wait in the chapel. "The doctor is on the way to see you. We can wait in here." Ok, so now I'm thinking to myself so why am I waiting in the chapel?

The chaplain went on to make small talk until finally I said, "So where is the doctor?" Seems like as soon as I asked the question, a middle aged looking woman with a stethoscope and lab coat walked in. She sat beside me and introduced herself as Dr. Creasy. "Ms. Williams, I am sorry to have to tell you this but your husband passed away this evening." As she continued to talk, I heard words like massive, heart, resuscitate, and autopsy coming from her mouth. I looked at her and said, "Excuse me? That is not possible. 39 year old people don't just die. Are you sure you have the right person?" I asked even though I knew in the pit of my stomach that what she was telling me was true. Dr. Creasy responded, "Yes, maam. Mr. Williams died at approximately 4:00 this evening. We were not able to revive him." And, in the blink of an eye, my life changed just like that.

17

LORD, I NEED YOU NOW

"Can I see him?" I was unbelievably calm considering the sudden massive shock that had just rocked my core. As Dr. Creasy led me to his room, I could see nurses and doctors looking at me as if "they knew." When I walked in the room, I saw Bernard lying there on his back just as handsome as ever. Maybe he was just sleeping I thought. Maybe it was just one horrible mistake. But as I got closer to him, it became increasingly and painfully clear that he wasn't just sleep, he was gone; gone from this earth, gone from this life, gone from me. No movement, no heart beat, just plain still. The tears fell as I touched his face, his heart, his hands. I said a small prayer to myself because for the life of me, I didn't know what else to do. I'd almost forgotten that

Dr. Creasy was in the room with me until she said, "Mrs. Williams, I need to ask you a few questions. I'll be back when you are ready."

I laid my head down on his chest and just held him. I can't truly explain how I felt other than pure shock and an overwhelming sense of heartache and dread. I laid there beside him saying over and over "God help me, God please help me." I just lay there listening to the rhythm of this constant sobbing. I didn't realize that sobbing was coming from me until I heard my mother say my name. I looked up and there she was standing there with my Aunt Max and Tammy. Them showing up and standing there just made it seem all more real. My sobbing then turned into a piercing scream like straight out of a horror movie.

When Bernard's family came, Dr. Creasy gave them the news just like she'd done with me. I'll never forget the look on his dad's face. A father losing his only son; the son that looked liked him, walked like him, talked like him. I don't think his dad was ever the same after that day. Just like you don't bury your husband at 35, you're not supposed to outlive and bury your young adult son either.

Before we left, Mr. Williams and I wanted to get one last look and say our goodbyes to Bernard before, well before the undertaker came and got him. It had gotten late and Bernard's fingers had started to turn blue. I remember Dr. Creasy saying

"It's time." Time for what? I thought. Time to take him away, time to drain his blood and make him up to look like some damn zombie, time for him to be buried in a deep dark grave, time for fucking what??? I kissed Bernard and took one last look. Bernard, my sweet Bernard.

The Williams' went back to D.C. that night, but my mom and I stayed in Hampton at my Aunt Max's house. I think I may have slept an hour that night, waking up around 4:00 the next morning. My eyes opened and I thought, damn that was a terrible dream. But, when I looked around the room and realized where I was and saw Tammy lying in the bed next to me, I immediately felt a burning sensation move throughout my body and that sense of dread that I felt last night came rushing back. This was no dream, this was real. The thought of that reality brought me to tears.

Tammy woke up around 6:30. I had been lying there almost all night with the TV on. Just the thought of being in the dark and in total silence freaked me out. I needed that distraction of the TV's light and sound. "Good morning. Were you able to get any sleep?" she asked me yawning all at the same time. "Not really," I said. She tried to make small talk but it was like I was there, but I wasn't. I could hear what she was saying but it was like she was talking to someone else and not me. Actually, it felt like that for the next several days, weeks, and months. The best way to describe it is an out of body experience.

It's as if my soul had left my body too, but I was still alive. The daze look is what I had and what I felt. I was in a freaking daze, stuck in a place that was dark, gloomy, scary, and fucking depressing.

The next couple of days were a mixture of calls and visits from everybody: work, church, friends, and family... "Is there anything I can do?" "You are still young, you'll get married again," "I'm sorry to hear about your loss", and my favorite "He's in a better place." What the hell? My 39 year old husband has been dead for like 3 minutes and folks are already telling me how I will find somebody else, and that he's in a better place. The place he needs to be is on this earth. I don't know where he is now. All I know is here on earth, and that's what I need is for Bernard to be here not somewhere "that's better"!! Oh, and I can't forget this one that I kept hearing, "God don't make mistakes." Ok, is it possible that He made a mistake this time?

I decided that the funeral would be in D.C. because that is where Bernard was from and where all of his family was. The Williams' had a family burial plot up there also in the Maryland area, so I thought it was best that Bernard be buried with his family. As we got closer to the day of the funeral, my mom and I rode up to Maryland to Bernard's dad's so that we could go see the body together. Uhhh, I hated when people called him "the body." It sounded so cold and just depressing. On the ride up, I thought about the last few days and all I had done like picking out Bernard's suit for the funeral and writing his obituary and outlining the funeral program. This time last week we were planning for the fourth of July weekend, and now I'm planning his funeral. Who plans their husband's funeral at age 35?

Ain't nothing worse than going to a funeral home. I sat in the car for as long as I could before I could muster up the courage to go inside. My mother and my dad were both with me. When we got up to Maryland, we stopped by my dad's house and picked him up. "I want to go with you baby girl," he had said when I had talked to him on the phone the night before. I was cool with that because I needed all of the support that I could get right about now, and having my daddy there with me made me feel safe somehow; safe from what, I don't know. Maybe safe from losing all control when I walked into this damn funeral home to view "the body."

Bernard's father and uncle were waiting for us when we got there. I started to feel a bit nauseous and faint as we walked down what seemed to be a long ass corridor. All I could think of was that Bernard was in here with all of these dead people. The funeral director and his assistant talked to us for awhile and asked a few questions before they led us to the room where Bernard was. "Again, Mrs. Williams, I am so sorry for your loss. If there is anything else that we can do for you, please let us know." "Can you bring him back?" I heard myself ask.

As we all walked in the room, I could see Bernard in that casket from a distance. I stopped and let his dad go on. I still felt a bit sick to my stomach, and this was just a tad bit too much to handle. My mom and dad both looked at each other not really knowing what to say to me. As my parents, all they wanted to do was to make everything right for me and to take my pain away. Unfortunately, it was nothing that they could do, nothing they could say. I had to do this, go through this, live it and survive it all on my own.

I saw Mr. Williams kiss Bernard on the cheek and walk away from the casket. As I walked up to where Bernard was, the last 15 years of my life with him started to flash before my eyes. I was afraid that he was going to look too dark, have way too much make-up, too thin, or too big, just look dead. You know some funeral homes do a jacked up job and you don't even recognize the person. To my surprise though, he looked like himself. He looked good. I was relieved.

On the morning of the funeral, I laid in the bed thinking about what the funeral would be like. I had only been to old people's funerals, so I didn't know what to expect. I couldn't imagine the number of people that would be there. Who would come?

In the midst of my thoughts, Tammy knocked on the door. "How are you doing this morning my friend?" She had insisted that I stay the last couple of nights with her. Actually, I had not stayed not one night at my house since Bernard died. "I'm hanging in there, but not looking forward to this at all," I said. "I know. I'm gonna be there right there with you, all of us will. I'm fixing a little breakfast so we can at least try to put something on our stomachs," she said and then stepped out. Nobody seemed to know what to say to me, and there was always this feeling of awkwardness whenever I would bring Bernard's name up. That would go on for weeks, even years later.

We had to drive up to D.C. for the funeral, so we got on the road about 9:00. We had to meet at my in law's house for the processional to the church. My mother, Aunt Max, Tammy, and I all rode together. Monica had flown into Baltimore from Chicago the night before. "Girl, I will meet you there tomorrow. Hang in there. I love you!" she had said when I talked to her on the phone the other night. I must say the whole ride to D.C. was a blur. I was burying the man that I loved since like forever today. I felt anxious, afraid, solemn, and alone; even with all of my closest loved ones around me, I still felt alone. Nothing prepares you for death, and certainly not a sudden one. How do you say good-bye when there were so many years of living left? He wasn't even 40 years old. People die at 89, not 39, right?

The church was packed. Cars everywhere on the outside. My daddy was standing out in front waiting for me. I felt like I wanted to loose it, but my daddy was right there holding me. For a brief minute, I felt like my daddy was going to make it all better like he did when I was a little girl. Reality set in quickly as we made our way in the church with me and my father in law leading the processional.

You could hear whimpers and sniffling when they closed Bernard's casket. That feeling of seeing your husband's casket close is one you truly never forget. You know that's the last time that you will ever see him, at least on this earth.

The service was actually good from what I can remember. I tried to be as focused as I possibly could because I wanted to be a part of his home going. So many people said so many wonderful things about Bernard. Family, friends, co-workers all had good words or funny stories that they shared. At one point, I looked down while I was blowing my nose, and I heard this familiar voice up at the microphone. I looked up, and there was Missy standing there. Yes, Missy was at my dead husband's funeral. She was up there at the mike with two other women, one young and one older. I just assumed it was her mother and sister. I turned to my father behind me and motioned with my lips, "That's her." He gave me a slight nod to indicate that he understood. Monica, who was sitting next to me, grabbed my hand and looked at me as if to say hold on girl, don't worry about that ho.

Missy didn't stay up there long thank goodness. She talked about how he had been friends with her and her family for years, how much they all cared about him, and how her daughter looked up to him. "My family loved him too," she said looking directly at me and then walked out. I looked over at Mr. Williams, and he looked away with his head down. Yeah these mother fucking Williams' family sitting up in here all knowing about and embracing this bitch for years. The nerve of her! How dare she show up at this funeral and get up and speak of all things! Well I guess she did what she came to do; to get her point across. I really couldn't even get mad for real because I had made my peace with Bernard and, at the end, we had chosen to be together. And really, he was dead now, so none of this truly didn't matter anymore. That was the last time that I saw or heard of Missy.

I think the burial was probably the most difficult of all of this. Going to that gravesite was a bit much too bare. Just the thought of leaving Bernard's body in that casket and being buried deep beneath the ground just seemed cold, dark, and dismal. It must be a better way to do say goodbye, this was just awfully depressing. Lord, if I ever needed you before, I need you now.

18

NO WEAPON FORMED AGAINST ME SHALL PROSPER

The next few weeks and months were rough. I stayed in that daze, that dark place, for what seemed like forever. Everybody else went back to their normal routine and the calls and visits became less and less. I didn't stay at home the first month, but knew I had to go back at some point. When I did, it felt cold and eerie. My Aunt Max said Bernard's spirit was still there and would be there until he felt that I was going to be ok. I swear I think she was a psychic in a previous life. Well, I'm not sure if I believed or wanted to believe in spirits lingering around or whatever, but there was definitely an unnatural, strange feeling about the house that lasted for weeks; so much so that I slept with the TV on until that strange feeling finally went away.

Dealing with the preparations of the funeral and the initial shock of Bernard's passing didn't even compare to the weeks and months that came afterwards. When Bernard died, I felt like I'd lost a part of myself. I felt alone, and like nobody understood the pain and range of emotions that I was going through. None of my friends or family could relate, and for the most part didn't know what to say to me or looked at me sometimes as if they thought I was going to lose it or something. They couldn't relate because they hadn't experienced losing a spouse at a young age, so there was no way that they could understand how deep that pain was.

Within a few weeks, I returned back to work and started my journey to getting back to "normal" too. It wasn't easy, but as time went on, the days, nights, weeks, and months did get a little easier. I kept praying. Even though I asked God, "Why Lord, why me, why now, why us" like a zillion times, I still never stopped going to church and praising Him. I also continued going to counseling. Dr. Washington was the best, and I owe a great deal of my healing to him. And looking at his fine ass a couple of times a month helped too I'm sure.

It took me another couple of years, but I finally finished up and received my doctorate. Yes, Dr. Caryn Williams, PHD! I moved to Charlotte, North

Carolina shortly thereafter accepting the President position at the University of Charlotte.

It was probably three years after Bernard died that I started and even wanted to start dating again. I couldn't imagine being with anyone else after losing him, but God, unbeknownst to me, had a plan for me.

I met Keith when I joined my church in Charlotte. He first caught my attention when he stood up and did his testimony at one evening service. He too had lost a wife at a young age. They were both 28 years old when she died. She was in a terrible car accident and was pronounced dead on the scene. After church, I told him that I also had lost a spouse and how I admired him for sharing his story in front of the congregation. From there, our relationship began.

Keith is everything that I could have ever dreamed of or asked for. He's a gentlemen, kind, loving, and respects the commitment of our relationship. Most of all, he truly loves me the way I deserve to be loved. Mature love. He's sexy as hell, and ok, he got money in his pocket and in the bank too. Hello! Thank you Jesus.

So, here I am putting flowers at Bernard's grave marking the five year anniversary of his death. Even though I am a newlywed now and love Keith dearly, I still think about Bernard often. It could be a song, a place, or a scent that reminds me of him. The feelings aren't really sad anymore, more like bittersweet. He was a part of my life for a long time, and those memories will always be a part of me. Someone asked me recently if I had any regrets. We all have regrets, don't we?

After everything I went through, I was able to make it through the worst storm of my life and finally get to my rainbow. People tell me all the time how strong I am and how they admire my strength. I can't take the credit. It was a whole lot of faith and a whole lot of crying that got me through it. Like the song goes, "No weapon formed against me shall prosper, it won't work..."

CPSIA information can be obtained
at www.ICGtesting.com
Printed in the USA
LVOW01s1245200816

501176LV00011B/219/P